A Christian Novel — Book 2

ROBERT HOLLOWAY

Falling Acorns
Copyright © 2023 by Robert Holloway

All rights reserved. No part of this publication may be reproduced, distributed, or transmitted in any form or by any means, including photocopying, recording, or other electronic or mechanical methods, without the prior written permission of the author, except in the case of brief quotations embodied in critical reviews and certain other non-commercial uses permitted by copyright law.

ISBN
978-1-960197-80-1 (Paperback)
978-1-960197-81-8 (eBook)

FALLING ACORNS
A sequel to *Deep Runs the River*

Dedication

This work of fiction is dedicated to our four children – Ralph, Lori, Ted. Susan – who have always been supportive of my varied interests and endeavors.

ACKNOWLEDGEMENTS

I am extremely grateful to Evelyn, my wife of fifty-six years, for her tolerance of my writing pursuits and for her critical eye and computer skills, which she has allowed me to call upon frequently. And those who have read the earlier manuscripts and offered valuable suggestions are greatly appreciated.

PREFACE

The road of life takes many twists and turns. The best laid plans sometimes go awry. The challenging climbs, the downward spirals, the defeats and the victories are all a part of the journey. Thankfully, most of the time the blessings and rewards are far greater than we imagine or deserve. Rusty Jenson experienced them all. As a rebellious, wayward youth he earned the reputation of being the "wild one," and got himself charged with attempted murder for which he spent five years of a seven-year sentence at Louisiana's Angola State Prison. Fortunately for him it was a blessing because there he was saved, received an education, and saw his life turned around. In time he returned home to Winslow to make amends for his wrongs only to learn after some time that he had been falsely accused of attempted murder after all and should never have been charged with more than disorderly conduct, public drunkenness, and fighting. However, undeterred he still sought to help the man he was accused of trying to kill, Ben Appleby, and his needy, though proud, family. Despite his good intentions and anonymous help, Rusty was met with rejection and hatred at every turn. In time, however, he gained the friendship and forgiveness of Ben and the entire Appleby family. In addition, he fell in love with Ben's sister Lauren, and despite his feelings of unworthiness, she accepted his proposal and agreed to marry him. After experiencing rejection after rejection in his job search, he was eventually blessed with a job he loved and at it he progressed up the ladder from doing the most menial jobs to become the foreman and eventually the owner of the company. He rose from utter rejection to overwhelming acceptance, from guilt to deliverance, from aloneness to family relationships, from crime to ministry, from poverty to financial security, but he recognized that he didn't do it alone. Others, especially his employer, Clark Howie, were very helpful, but most of all Rusty gave God the credit for the miraculous things in his life.

May this sequel to "Deep Runs the River" be a blessing to you.

CHAPTER 1

Rusty followed Pastor Williams out of the side door into the sanctuary and marched to his place before the altar. Clark Howie, Rusty's employer and friend, followed him and took his place beside him. A moment later Cathy, the bride's sister, came slowly down the aisle and stood on the opposite side. When the "Wedding March" began, the large congregation of friends stood to their feet and turned to face the bride as she came forward. The most beautiful woman Rusty had ever seen came gracefully down the aisle wearing a gorgeous wedding gown to meet him at the altar, but what caught everyone's attention was not just the bride but the man who ushered her down the aisle. It was her only brother, Ben, the paraplegic in his wheel chair. Lauren's hand rested on his shoulder as they came slowly down the aisle. When the wedding party was assembled at the front of the church, the pastor asked, "Who gives this woman to be married to this man?" Ben answered proudly, "Her mother, sister, and I." As he motored to his reserved spot, Rusty moved to stand beside Lauren and take her hand in his. She was so proud of this tall, handsome man with rusty, red hair. In his black tux one hardly noticed the rugged weathered face and the calloused hands of a working man. After a brief message about the sacredness of marriage, scripture reading, and prayer, came the question Rusty had long waited to answer: "Rusty Jenson do you take Lauren Appleby to be you wedded wife?"

"I sure do," he said with a little too much gusto, causing a low snicker to spread through the audience. When Lauren had also pledged her love and faithfulness to Rusty with a soft "I do," they turned to face each other to recite the vows they had separately written themselves. Rusty spoke first:

"Lauren, I think I've loved you since the first time I saw you, but I never thought you could come to love one as unworthy as I felt. As I've been able to get to know you better, my love for you has grown to be more than I can describe. I, therefore, promise to love you without reservation, to be a partner to you in our marriage, to accept your family as mine, and to be faithful to you for the rest of my life. And I give you this ring as a token of my love." With that, He placed the ring on her finger.

Then it was Lauren's turn and with tears flowing down her face, she said, "Rusty, once when I didn't know you I hated you for what I thought you did to my brother, but now I have come to love you more than anything else. I have seen that your compassion, your faith in God, and your sacrificial service to God and man are without limits. Therefore, I know that you are more than worthy of my love. I feel honored to give it. It's because of you that I am a Christian and can be equally yoked together with you today in marriage. I now give myself to you to be a partner in life and in whatever endeavors we undertake. I'll forsake all others to be faithful to you in every way so long as I shall live. And I put this ring on your finger to always reflect the union that we are forming."

"Amen," the pastor said. "And now it gives me great pleasure to exercise the authority vested in me by the laws of this state and looking to heaven for divine sanction, to pronounce you husband and wife. Rusty, you may kiss your bride."

Rusty kissed his bride a little more passionately than was expected, causing a pink blush to her face; then they turned to exit up the aisle, and Pastor Williams said, "Ladies and gentlemen, I present to you Mr. and Mrs. Rusty Jenson." Everyone rose to their feet clapping, while the ladies dabbed tears from their eyes. Slowly they all made their way to the beautifully decorated fellowship hall for a reception with plenty of congratulations, well wishes and hugs, as well as ample food. An hour later, with the license signed and witnessed, the Jensons made their way toward their decorated car to drive the short distance to their new house. Even though Rusty was prepared to go anywhere for their honeymoon, Lauren had requested they spend their honeymoon at home.

Marriage is always a union of two people pledging to become one in marriage. But marriage is seldom just two; it also involves new in-laws, former relationships, the spouse's friends, and sometimes children from previous marriages. For Lauren and Rusty it meant a family relationship with her entire family, all four of them. Rusty's remaining family was lost to him; he didn't even know where they were because they had long since given up on their wayward brother. So Lauren's family had become his family in every sense of the word. According to his plans they would share more than a kinship; they would be a family, sharing a home and life together.

According to Rusty's plans, Marie Appleby, Ben, and Cathy went home to begin packing for their move, and a week later Rusty and Lauren came with movers to take them to their new home. Rusty and Lauren had insisted that Marie quit her job so she could stay home with Ben and live in the apartment Rusty had included for them in his house plans. Ben had not seen the house before, and when he saw his bedroom with a built-in lift, and his own specially-equipped bathroom, he was awestruck. Marie had all of the equipment she needed to cook, watch television and sleep in their own apartment separate from the newlyweds, but Rusty and Lauren insisted that they all share their meals and time together as a family. Cathy, who occupied one of the spare bedrooms, was delighted with her space for studying, sitting, and sleeping, and especially with her own private bath.

The next week everyone went about their routine. Marie was given a weekly stipend, and access to the family checkbook to cover any household expenses so she shopped for groceries, cooked their meals, cleaned the house, and took care of Ben. Rusty returned to his work at Clark's Woodworking, and Lauren went back to the TLC Nursing Home where she was the head nurse. Cathy went back to school to finish her degree in physical therapy. Every one was happy with the arrangement. After years of living in a small rented house, the Applebys were grateful for a comfortable home, and Rusty was thrilled to provide it. A little time would be needed to adjust to their new arrangements, but everyone was more than willing to make it work.

About a week after they had settled in the new house, Lauren nudged Rusty from a sound sleep to ask, "What is that noise?"

"What noise?" he mumbled.

"Listen and you will hear it, sleepy head." He did, but he couldn't tell what it was either, so he went to the back door and looked out and listened.

"The mystery is solved," he said when he returned to the bed. "You remember that large oak tree we left growing near the back of the house? Well, the wind is blowing acorns from it and they are falling on the house."

"Okay, we can put up with that as long as I know what it is," Lauren responded.

It was only a year later that Cathy graduated and began working at the local hospital where one of her first patients was an engineer with a passion for Harleys. Having been in an accident he had come to her for physical therapy but it soon grew into more than professional services. By the time the therapy was finished they were madly in love and he was begging her to marry him. Soon she said "yes," and after a short engagement they were married and Cathy moved out of the Jenson house and into his apartment.

More good news came when Lauren discovered that she was pregnant. The whole family was delighted, Ben even more when Rusty told him that if it was a boy they would name him Benji after him. That would be eight months away and lots could happen before then, and it did. Ben had not been doing well, but because he had no feeling below his neck, he couldn't tell if he was having any pain or not. However, Lauren noticed that his color was not good and that he was not eating well, so she knew that it was time to see a doctor and do some testing. After a week in the hospital and having just about every test available, the doctor requested the family to come for a conference. "I'm sorry to have to tell you," he began. Marie burst into tears and cried, "Oh, no!" When she calmed down enough to listen, the doctor continued, "Ben has bone cancer."

"How bad is it?" Lauren wanted to know.

"It's advanced to stage four, I'm afraid."

"What can we do for him?" Rusty inquired.

"Because of his other health issues, I don't advise any treatment. It would be too hard on him and, in my opinion, do little good. We can try to keep him comfortable and make the most of his remaining time, but that's about all," the doctor said grimly.

"Doctor, how long do you think he has?" Marie asked.

"At best a few months, maybe less. I'm sorry."

As Ben's health deteriorated, Lauren wanted to move him to the nursing home, but Marie balked. "He is my son, and I intend to take care of him. I want him to live out his life with the family who loves him, not among strangers." Lauren acquiesced, but arranged for around-the-clock nurses to help with him at home. When Rusty and Lauren learned they were going to have a boy, they told Ben that he was going to have a namesake and he was thrilled.

After giving Ben a few days to contemplate his impending death, Rusty asked him to keep him informed of what he was feeling. Lauren had told him that it helped to talk about one's illness and approaching death instead of ignoring the subject, but she didn't think she would be able to keep her emotions intact to talk with Ben about it. So Rusty sat with him regularly and they talked about how Ben felt, what pain he was feeling, and how he felt about dying. "Well, Rusty, I'm not anxious to die, but neither am I afraid of dying. My future is as secure as the promises of God. I really don't have much to live for here, just life in this chair. I hate the thought of leaving my family but I have much to anticipate after death. Just think, I'll be able to walk again and I'll have lots of new friends; I won't need this chair anymore. You can find someone else who needs one but can't afford it and give it to them."

"Thanks Ben. I'm glad you can feel that way. We will surely miss you, but until that time comes we are going to do the best we can to take care of you, so if you need anything be sure to let us know."

"I'm grateful. You know, Rusty, you've been a lot better to me already than I deserve. I never had a brother, but you are like one to me. And just think, I once hated you, and now I can truly say that I love you." Every few days Rusty and Ben talked for it did seem to help to talk about what Ben was facing. Every day he seemed to grow weaker, and one night as they talked Ben said, "Rusty, I'm sorry that I won't live to see my nephew, but I'm sure he will be fine. Could you ask the rest of the family to come in here?" They called Cathy and the whole family gathered around Ben's bed. He struggled to say to them, "I want to thank you all for what you have done for me. I'm sorry that I have been such a burden to you. Now I want to say goodbye to all of you while I still can. I don't know how long I have to live but I don't think it will be long. I don't want you to be sad; after all, I'm prepared to die now, thanks to my Christian brother-in-law and sisters. Rusty, will you lead us in prayer?"

Rusty hesitated to speak at first, trying to get his emotions under control, but as everyone cried he managed to praise God and thank Him for saving Ben and sustaining him through the years since his injury. He asked God to make his passing from this life pleasant and to give the family members the grace they would need to overcome their loss when the time came. No one noticed but during the prayer Ben just stopped breathing. With tears streaming down her cheeks, Lauren examined him. She knew there was no need to try CPR or to rush him to the emergency room at the hospital. Instead, after they had stood around his bed and kissed him goodbye she covered him with the sheet and called the coroner who came and pronounced him dead. The funeral home personnel came and took the body away and made an appointment to meet with them at ten the next morning to finalize the funeral arrangements.

Marie and Lauren insisted that Rusty deliver the eulogy at Ben's funeral service. Although he had never done so before, he agreed to try. For two days he wrestled with the task of formulating an appropriate message. Finally, with Marie, Lauren, and Cathy's consent, he chose to share Ben's story. "Like me, Ben was a rebel," Rusty began. "We disappointed our families, wasted our youth, and brought trouble on ourselves with alcohol and drugs. In a barroom brawl, which Ben initiated, he was injured for life, left a paraplegic. His family sacrificed greatly to provide him with the best of care constantly. Even though he was difficult to deal with at first, thinking that nobody could love him, he came to the realization that God loved him and that He would give him new life if he called on Him in faith. So, after trusting Christ as his Savior, Ben came to know the happiest days of his life and recognize how much his family loved him. So as we come to say goodbye to him today, we do so knowing that he was prepared to meet the Lord and that he is well and secure for all eternity." Walking down from the pulpit to face the casket, Rusty ended his comments with, "So long, Ben. We will see you soon."

In that casket Ben looked as if he had no infirmity; in fact, he looked like he was about to speak. A blanket of beautiful floral arrangements covered the grave at the cemetery and when everyone else had offered their condolences and assistance, the family stood by the grave and Marie said, "Life will be different for all of us now. I don't know what I'll do with myself.... Oh yes I do, I'll be busy being a nanny for my new grandchild. And I can hardly wait."

The time was drawing near for the birth of the baby, so a few days before the due date, Marie sat with Rusty and Lauren and told them, "I have a request. I would like to be the baby's nanny. With Ben gone I have little to do, and I need to be busy, so there is nothing I'd like better than to care for my first grandchild, and anymore that come along," she added with a smile.

"If you are sure, Mom. There is nothing we would like better, but we don't want to impose on you. Rusty and I have discussed it but we didn't want to be the ones to suggest it because we thought maybe you needed a rest from all the hard work you've been doing," Lauren responded.

"It won't be work for me to love on my first grandchild," she insisted.

"You know we have equipped the nursery, but if there is anything else we will need you let us know. You know lots more about this than we do."

"Rusty, Rusty," Lauren called out as she shook the sleeping man beside her.

"Huh? What? What is it?"

"Wake up, you're about to be a father."

Rusty jumped right out of bed, dressed hurriedly and said, "Let's go."

Lauren was barely out of bed, pausing every few minutes to allow another contraction to pass. "Wait for me, silly. We don't have to rush. You'll have hours to wait and walk the floor. Go wake Mom and call Cathy and tell them we're going to the hospital. They'll probably want to come too." In the car, Rusty was so excited that he turned on the flashers, exceeded the speed limit, and ran all of the red lights as if it were some immediate emergency. Soon after their arrival, Marie and Cathy rushed in and asked what was going on. Walk the floor Rusty did. And every few minutes he asked Marie, "Do you think something is wrong?" He must have checked his watch every two minutes until six hours later when a smiling nurse came out with an eight-pound baby boy wrapped in a warm blanket and placed the infant in his father's arms. "Is Lauren okay?" he asked. Once he was assured that she was fine, he beamed as he held the infant awkwardly. After a few minutes, Marie had to ask if Rusty was going to allow them to hold the baby too, and reluctantly, he handed him over just as the nurse came to get him and take him back to his mother.

When Lauren came home with the baby two days later, and Marie called them to dinner, Rusty insisted that they put Benji in his carrier and bring him also and set him right on the table. After a delicious meal of vegetables and Swiss steak, Rusty announced that he wanted all of them to agree that they would gather for dinner every night at 6:00 p.m., and that following the meal they would read from the Bible and pray each time. "I want Benji to grow up in a devout Christian environment." He knew that both he and Lauren would sometimes have work to do after dinner, but they could always take a break to meet for dinner. There would surely be changes in their lives and he wanted them to all be positive.

Rusty took lots of teasing at work about the new arrival and how it would change his life, but he was about the proudest father any one of the crew had ever seen. Pictures of the newborn were taped to the office walls, and they were replaced with new, up-to-date ones every week. True to his word, no matter what happened at work, Rusty was home at 6:00 for dinner. Invariably, he brought Benji to the table for dinner, the Bible reading, and prayer.

CHAPTER 2

As soon as Lauren felt up to it, she and Rusty took the baby to show him to the Howies, who were delighted to see him as well as his parents. "You know, Rusty," Clark began, "it would be mighty easy to worship a little one like that."

"I'm sure you are right, Clark, but I just want to love him with my whole heart and reserve my worship for the only One who deserves it, and that is my Lord." Silently he prayed that God would always allow him to do both.

Even though Eva Howie's condition was growing worse daily, Clark was still trying to care for her on his own for twenty-four hours a day. Finally, exhausted, he decided to hire sitters to help, but was disappointed with their service. "'Sitters' is all most of them are,"

he complained. Others were not always dependable either; they either didn't show up for work, or one of them was always quitting, so they were required to learn new people and acquaint them with Eva's needs and their home every few days. Finally, as a last resort, Clark talked to Lauren about moving Eva to the nursing home where she would have twenty-four-hour care by better trained professionals. Most of all he wanted Lauren's expert oversight and care for Eva. So for the rest of her life Eva was cared for at TLC Nursing Home, but Clark was as faithful to her as ever. Every day he was with her from noon until she was asleep at night. Despite excellent care, in the months ahead her health deteriorated steadily. Then one morning when Lauren was making her usual rounds, beginning with Eva, as she always did, she found her eyes wide open in death. After examining her, she quickly called Clark and he came immediately. Lauren, as well as staff members offered what comfort they could, but poor Clark was devastated. He was given a few minutes alone with her before the coroner and funeral home personnel were called. Then when he came out of her room to join Lauren, he sobbed, "I don't know how I can go on living without her." After all, they had enjoyed fifty years of happy marriage together.

Clark looked as if he might not make it through the memorial service at which Rusty and Pastor Williams spoke. Even worse were the days at home following the funeral. Rusty and some other friends went by every day to check on him and try to comfort him, but it looked like he would grieve himself to death, and, in fact, he lived only a few months. The doctor said he could find no cause of death other than a broken heart.

To Rusty's surprise, Clark's lawyer called about ten days later and asked him to be present for the reading of Clark's will the next morning at 10:00. Having never been a party to such things, Rusty had no idea why he needed to be present. Pastor Williams was already there when Rusty arrived at 10:00 and Rusty couldn't imagine why he would need to be there either. "Good morning gentlemen," Attorney Albertson greeted them. "If you are ready, we will get to this matter. As you know Clark was the kind of man who took care of business, leaving no loose ends. So you would guess that he left a detailed will and that you are both named in it. Clark left a sizeable estate, and he left it to the things and people that meant the most to him. Pastor, to First Church he is leaving one-third of his entire estate. And he has designated one-third of it to fund a foundation honoring Eva. Regarding that bequeath, he has left a note of instructions for Rusty. He requests that you, Rusty, administer the foundation and that its primary purpose is to open and operate one or more halfway houses to aid in moving those who are coming out of prison back into mainstream society. He states that he feels he made a wise decision in taking you in and giving you a job, and that because of your experience you are the best suited to help others. Furthermore, he leaves the houses he and Eva and his parents occupied for immediate use as halfway houses. He suggests that they can be modified as you wish to house fifteen to twenty occupants. He also states specifically that he is not burdening you with the day-to-day operation of the facilities. So you are to employ other suitable people to do that, but he requests that you have regular times when you can meet with the residents and guide them on the right path. He also asks that his portion of the profits from Clark's Woodworking be channeled into the foundation. Finally, Rusty, the last one-third is left to you with no strings attached."

"What? I'm shocked!" Rusty exclaimed. "He has always been so good to me during his life that I could never expect any more after his death."

Albertson added, "We are talking about approximately $750,000 to be divided three ways. And let me make it clear that you are to abide by the stipulations in the will. As his named executor, I'll receive regular reports from you and make sure that his wishes are carried out, and they had better be."

"We shall do as he says, I assure you, Sir," the pastor said. Then he added, "Thank you, Clark. Watch over us as we use these funds wisely." In the days ahead, Rusty wondered what he was to do with his portion of the money. He knew he could never use it selfishly for himself, so he promised the deceased benefactor that it would go to some good cause.

A week later an old model ford rattled into the parking lot at Clark's Woodworking and an older man with three day's growth of beard ambled into the shop and asked to see Mr. Jenson. He was directed to Rusty and when they had introduced themselves he asked if they could talk in private. Rusty assumed that he was just another man down on his luck asking for a handout, but he took him into the office to hear his story. "I'm Marlon Howie," he began. "Clark Howie was my cousin, and I didn't know he'd died. I didn't even get to come and pay my last respects," he said, tearing up.

"I'm sorry about the loss of your relative," Rusty replied. "I've known Clark for a number of years but I never heard him mention any close relatives."

"Oh yes," Marlon added. "His father and mine were first cousins. I figure that makes me a forced heir to his estate, so I've come to claim my part of it."

"Well, Marlon, " Rusty said finally, " the estate has been divided as Clark planned it in his will, but I don't believe your name was in it. I'm sure that if he had wanted you to have part of his estate he would have named you."

"But I am entitled to some of it," Marlon argued. "And if I have to I'll go to court to get it I will. I figure since you seem to have plenty, with this shop and all, you could save yourself a lot of trouble and lawyer fees if you would voluntarily give me say $100,000 of the money. I hear the church got a good part of it but I don't want to trouble the good pastor for any. How about it?"

"Marlon, I don't even know if you are related to Clark. But the most important thing is that Clark's will is being carried out perfectly, so I'm afraid I can't go against his wishes."

"I would think to ensure the safety of your family you would grant my request," Howie mumbled.

"What do you know about my family?" Rusty demanded angrily.

"Well, I know where you live. I know you have a little boy and that your wife is a nurse at the TLC Nursing Home. I know that you wouldn't want any of them to be harmed," Marlon said.

Rusty was infuriated. "Are you threatening my family?" he demanded. Rusty knew what to do to this bum and that he could easily handle him, but to be safe he said, "Let me call my attorney and ask him about it, Marlon." When the lawyer got on the line, Rusty told him what had been said.

"You keep him right there and I will see you in a few minutes," Albertson said. Only a few minutes elapsed before the chief of police, dressed in a business suit and driving an unmarked car arrived, followed by the attorney. After introductions were made, the policeman had Rusty to tell him what had been said; then he turned to Marlon who looked like all of the blood had drained from his face by then; "Sir, you are under arrest for threatening this man's family. Put your hands behind your back."

"I wasn't going to harm them. It was just talk," Marlon pleaded. "Please don't lock me up; I have a family to provide for. I'll leave now if you'll let me go," Marlon pleaded.

The attorney added, "You can also be charged with attempted fraud. Even if you were kin to Clark, you have no claim on his estate and to claim otherwise is a crime." His old car was left on the parking lot when the police chief took him to the city jail and held him for three days.

Then Rusty went to see the chief of police and asked what could be done about him. "Well, we can't hold him, since no crime was actually committed. I think we could free him, but tell him that we will hold this charge and that if he causes any more trouble we will activate it," the chief responded.

"Okay. Can I talk with him before you release him?" Rusty asked.

"Certainly. Come on, I'll take you to his cell. This place doesn't smell the best, so be prepared," he said.

Rusty went back into the jail primarily to witness to the man who called himself Marlon Howie and to try to lead him to faith in the Lord. Belligerent at first, Marlon soon broke down and confessed how wrong he had been and how sorry he was. His name wasn't even Howie. He didn't know Clark, but he had read the legal news and thought he saw a chance to get some money that he really needed for his family. He had come from Arkansas and swore that if he could get out of jail he would go straight back there and cause no more trouble.

Before allowing him to be released, Rusty presented the claims of scripture and urged him to receive Christ and be saved. Then, following Rusty's lead, he prayed the sinner's prayer to be forgiven and saved. "If I arrange for your release," Rusty asked, "what will you do?"

"If I had gas money I would go home to Arkansas and begin to live a new life," he swore. So Rusty asked for his release, drove him back to his car, gave him $50.00, and sent him on his way.

CHAPTER 3

In a couple of weeks Lauren returned to work and began to notice how drab the place looked. She thought about the bright, lively colors of their nursery at home and wondered if old people would not like something beautiful too. So she called Mr. Wilson, the owner of the home, one day and asked him to come by at his convenience. When he did she began to suggest that the facilities needed improvements and redecorating. She suggested new trends in elderly care and what they would need to do to get on board. "The competition is already getting ahead of us in the services and facilities they offer, and they are getting the residents too," she suggested.

"That will cost a lot of money, young lady," Wilson replied.

"Yes, I know it will," she admitted, "but I think these people deserve the best we can give them and they are not getting it now. If you are not willing to upgrade you will lose money in the long run," Lauren argued.

"You know I'm getting old too, and I don't need to take on a lot of debt. This place doesn't make me a lot of money, but I'll think about it and get back with you," he promised. When she had not heard from him in a week, Lauren called him again and learned that he was still thinking about it. The next week she called him again. He seemed a little agitated that she wouldn't drop the matter, but said, "I'll tell you what, young lady, I think I have a solution to this problem, and if it's all right with you I'll be there tomorrow at 10:00 to tell you about it."

"That will be perfect, Mr. Wilson. And thank you, Sir," Lauren said.

As promised, Wilson showed up the next day at 10:00 sharp. Lauren began with an apology: "Mr. Wilson, I'm sorry if I've been pushing you so much for this and making a nuisance of myself. It's just that I feel so strongly about it."

"I gathered as much," he responded. "And I must say, Lauren, that from all I've heard you are the best person we have ever employed here in any capacity. You seem to be a great advocate for seniors. I would certainly want you on my side if I were a patient here. Now for my proposal, let me lease you TLC."

"Oh, Mr. Wilson, I don't know if that's possible." Lauren responded. "I don't know if I can manage to do all that is necessary to run this home. I'm trained to be a nurse, and if I must say so myself, I'm good at that, but I don't know much about business or administration. I don't think I can do it," Lauren answered.

"Yes, you can" he responded, "because you have what it takes. You see, the difference between you and me is that I'm a businessman and this is a for-profit business. I'm hands off of the actual administration and care, just paying someone else to operate it and do all of the work, and I just collect the profits. But you care about the patients more than the dollars and that is what they need. Unfortunately, I haven't been that way and I'm too old to change now. What do you say?"

"I don't know, Mr. Wilson. I would love to do it, but I have very little money. Tell me what kind of deal you are proposing," Lauren responded.

"I will give you a long-term lease for $5,000 a month, and you will have free reign in re-

decorating and making upgrades. You can do whatever you want then," Wilson offered.

"Who will pay for maintenance and upgrades?" Lauren asked wisely.

"Well, I figure that will be your responsibility."

"I don't think that will work, Mr. Wilson, but let me think about it."

When he had gone Lauren walked down the hall to speak with the financial secretary.

"What is the monthly profit at TLC?" she asked.

"Mr. Wilson does not allow me to give out that kind of information, but why do you need to know?" Lauren then told her about Mr. Wilson's offer and explained that she was simply investigating the feasibility of it.

"Turning to her computer, the secretary pulled up the information and answered, "For the past year, Mr. Wilson has received about $4,000 a month, but don't tell him that I told you, please."

"I see," Lauren responded. "Thank you for the information." Mr. Wilson was eager to get Lauren's answer, so he came two days later and asked if she had made a decision.

"Yes, I have. I'm sorry, Sir, but I can't possibly do that." She didn't want to report that one of his employees had violated his instructions and given her the information, so she didn't tell him why she couldn't accept the deal.

A week later, Mr. Wilson was back to see Lauren. "Look," he began "if you are not willing to rent, then let me sell this place to you."

"I don't know, Sir. I don't know if I could afford it and I don't know if I could even borrow the money. In addition to the selling price, I would need to spend a lot to improve the place and bring it up to standard. The state inspector has already said that we have to make some major changes. But, tell me, how much are you thinking about asking for TLC?" Lauren asked out of curiosity.

With a greedy gleam in his eyes, Wilson said, "I'll let it go for a bargain at a million dollars. But, remember, I'm willing to finance it for you."

"What kind of interest would you charge?"

"Just ten percent."

Tired of the game Wilson was playing, Lauren said, "I can tell you for sure right now that it isn't worth nearly that much, and if I were buying it, I can get a much better rate of interest at the bank." Lauren stated emphatically.

"Oh, I don't believe that. Just how much do you think it should go for?" the owner asked.

"I don't know anything about its value, but with the shape it is in I don't think it would be even half that much," Lauren said.

"You must be crazy," he charged. "That's a lot less than I can take, so I guess we will have to continue as we have been," Wilson complained.

"No, Sir. The state is not going to let us do that. Listen, Mr. Wilson, if you really want to sell, the fairest thing for both of us is that we get an objective, out-of-town appraiser to come and give us a figure of its value. Then we can go from there," she suggested.

That very afternoon, Ken Phillips, the state inspector showed up at the home. He already had information about the home and changes that would have to be made, so he simply reported that state guidelines required complete redecoration, new kitchen equipment, several items of new equipment, an examination room, a whirlpool bath, new bedding, and more employees. Lauren couldn't see beyond the dollar signs, knowing that if she bought the home that cost would fall on her. Phillips left his report to be passed on to the owner, with instructions that the work must begin within three months.

When Wilson received the report he was furious and thought that he would use his political influence to circumvent the regulations, so he called his state senator and representative and after getting no help with them, he called the governor and demanded to be exempt from the regulations and that Phillips be replaced.. "I'm sorry, but that's what the U.S. government requires and we can do no less," the governor replied. Then he contacted his national representatives but again, without success.

The very next day, Wilson strutted into the nursing home and said to Lauren, "Okay, you win. I'll agree to the appraisal, but I think you will be surprised. You be sure that you don't get some cousin to do the appraisal. I'll want to approve whomever you engage, and you will have to pay him."

"I can agree to that," she said. He'll probably be a lot more surprised than I will, she thought.

"Understand, Mr. Wilson, I have to discuss this with my husband. And I'll need to pray and seek God's will. And while I'm at it," she added, with a smile, "I'm going to pray that you will be willing to do the right thing. I'll call you when the appraisal is done."

With that Mr. Wilson left mumbling under his breath.

That evening Lauren asked Rusty and Marie to discuss something with her and give her their opinions. She told them about Mr. Wilson's offer and agreement that they get an appraisal, but assured them that she wanted their advice and God's leadership in the matter. "Let's pray about it right now," Rusty suggested. So they bowed their heads and asked God's to show them what to do.

With their encouragement, Lauren hired an appraiser, who came highly recommended, from a town fifty miles away. He inspected the building, checked the financial records, and examined the state inspector's report to learn what changes were needed and the approximate cost. Two weeks later he presented her with the completed report and offered to be present to answer any of Mr. Wilson's questions. Lauren then called Wilson and asked him to come the next day to discuss the matter, but she knew that he would not be happy with an appraisal of less than half the asking price. That evening, she discussed the matter with the family again. "The appraisal is $290,000, but we will need more for improvements. I don't know if we could borrow that much money or if we even want to. It would be so much better if that old skinflint would just make the necessary changes himself."

"I know where we can get some of the money," Rusty offered. " I've been waiting for some good cause to use money Clark left us, and I can't think of a better use. If we use it we will not have to borrow nearly as much."

"Are you sure about that Rusty?" Lauren asked. "After all, that's your money."

"Yes, I'm certain," Rusty answered, "I don't think I could ever use that money selfishly, but I would be glad to put it to use in this way if God wants us to do this. And listen, you remember that what's mine is yours too. I know you love that place and that you would improve it greatly."

"Do we know for sure that it is God's will?" Lauren asked.

"What if we ask God for a sign?" Rusty asked. "It will be a miracle if Mr. Wilson agrees to sell for that amount. So let's ask God if He wants us to do it, He will have Mr. Wilson to agree to the appraised price. Let's agree that we won't negotiate. If God wants us to have it, He will make it work."

With everyone in agreement, they waited for the meeting the next morning. A few minutes after ten Mr. Wilson showed up at the home. And, knowing there would be questions about the appraisal, the appraiser, Mark Allison, came also. "Well, what's the good news?" Mr. Wilson asked. Mark handed him the finished appraisal, several pages long. "Just give me the bottom line," Wilson insisted.

"The bottom line is $290,000, Sir," Mark responded.

"You must be out of your mind! That's not good news." Wilson yelled. "This can't be right! How did you arrive at this figure?" he demanded.

Patiently, Mark went through the appraisal process, showing him the value of the physical property, the estimated expenses of updating it to comply with state regulations, and the anticipated income. "Lauren, I think you need to get another appraisal," Wilson grumbled.

"No, Mr. Wilson," she said, "if you want another appraisal, you will have to get it and pay for it. My family and I have agreed that we will pursue this only if you agree to this price. If you do, then we will consider it a sign from God that we are supposed to buy it."

"What will you compromise for? Say $700,000?" Wilson enquired

"No, Sir. The appraisal amount is our final offer," Lauren answered stubbornly.

"If I accept this, will you let me finance it at ten percent interest?"

"No, Sir. I'm afraid not. We have most of the money and, therefore, we will not need a loan from you, but thanks for the offer," Lauren responded.

"And what if I keep it and refuse to make the expensive changes?" Wilson asked.

"Phillips said you have three months to begin or it will be shut down."

"Okay, if you insist on stealing it from me, I guess I'll have to accept it, Wilson conceded. "That's $290,000 to be paid in full. Is that correct?"

"Yes, Sir. Shall I get Mr. Albertson to begin the paper work?" Lauren asked.

"Yeah, go ahead, I guess."

"Thank you, Mr. Wilson. I intend to make this a home you'll be glad to live in when you need to."

"I hope I never need to," he grumbled.

CHAPTER 4

The next morning at breakfast after Lauren's sleepless night, Rusty asked her, "How do you feel about the nursing home purchase now?"

"I'm scared to death. I wasn't able to sleep last night for thinking about it. I'm afraid I might be taking on more than I can handle, but I kept remembering what John Wayne reportedly said: 'Courage is being scared to death but saddling up anyway.'"

"Well, if it doesn't work out, we can always blame God," Rusty said with a chuckle.

"What do you mean?"

"We asked God to give us a sign and He gave it. Now all we have to do is trust that He knows what He is doing and that He will make a way for us to follow His will." Rusty argued convincingly.

"I know. I'm sorry for worrying." Lauren apologized. " I'll just have to do lots of praying and trusting Him."

Lauren began immediately to outline her plans for TLC. Her dream was to renovate the entire building and get rid of the "institutional" look and paint it with bright, lively colors, such as yellow, blue, green, and red. She wanted to create a family atmosphere which she hoped to do by enlarging the commons area and making it a family room large enough to seat most of the residents at once. Those who were able would be brought to the family room every morning, and then again after their afternoon naps. She had a real burden for Alzheimer patients and felt that it was not the best treatment for them to be isolated in some special unit, so she intended to bring them, at least those whose illness had not progressed too far, into the main family of the home and expose them to lucid residents and involve them in the family life. To do so a good security system would have to be installed which would control the flow of traffic in and out. Some well-trained pets and life-like dolls would be brought into the family room for patients to enjoy. She thought maybe she could borrow some of the old family pictures which patients had and display them on the walls. That might help them feel at home. To begin to accomplish her goals, Lauren knew that she would need to provide better training for the staff and she began making plans to bring in medical experts, especially those involved in senior care, to train her employees and to improve their care of the residents. Knowing that most seniors had been involved in gardening, either of vegetables or flowers, she planned to prepare a garden spot for those who wished to putter in it. In addition to all of this she knew she would have to upgrade the equipment and facility to meet the state requirements. For the present all she could see was a long, expensive process, but remembering what Jesus said, "Don't worry about tomorrow, because tomorrow will worry about itself. Each day has enough trouble of its own" (Matthew 6:34 HCSB), she decided they would take just one step at a time.

When a line of credit was secured at the bank and the money handed over to Mr. Wilson and the papers signed, Lauren knew that she was in charge and felt the burden of it. She first met with the administrator and office personnel and informed them of the change in ownership but encouraged them not to publicize it. She wanted them to be aware that, while remaining as the head nurse, she would own and direct the overall operation of TLC. The administrator would continue to do her job, but under Lauren's supervision. "We will strive to make this the best home in town for seniors. I have several changes in mind and while I hope you all will be happy with them, if you are not, we will part as friends. If we have more staff than we need, it will be trimmed, but if we need more, we will try to provide them. However, you will be required to justify any additional employees."

Next, Lauren met with each shift of the nursing personnel and aides. She informed them that changes were in the making and that they would be a major part of the improvements. She went down her list as it affected them and emphasized that their first responsibility would be a good attitude and the best of care for the residents. She informed them that she expected them to see the patients as people whose needs would be foremost. Ignoring calls for help, mistreatment of residents, and failure to provide prompt care would not be tolerated. "We are going to demand more of you, so if you can't accept that, we will accept your resignation with regrets; however, those who do accept it and give their best, can expect a sizeable increase in pay. We will also provide monthly in-service training. No longer will we hire someone right off the street and start them in service without any training. Furthermore, we cannot tolerate absenteeism without just cause. If you fail to show up for work without first notifying us and giving us time to get someone to take your responsibilities you will be asked to resign. We will not permit anything that will impact negatively on our residents."

An aide raised her hand and asked, "How can we meet the needs of demanding patients who can never be satisfied.?"

"We will find a way. First, we will begin to see them as residents in our home, not patients in an institution. If one is constantly calling for attention when no real need exists, we will experiment to see how we can satisfy them. We will offer a lady a doll and ask her to take care of it or put a dog in her lap to pet. The key is to find out what is really wrong and seek to correct it. We will have soothing music at all times, very little television, and guest programs by volunteers. We will place round tables in the family room and put board games on them for residents' use. Seniors like children, so we will get children to visit the home and junior high school students to read to the residents, so if you have either of those you might try to bring them here sometime. We will have an ombudsman to act as a laison between the patients and the staff, to help us alleviate any problems and provide the best care possible. We hope to have an organization of volunteers to assist in whatever way they can. Now, for this kind of service, we know that we will have to charge the residents a little more, but we are going to make our home worth it."

Next Lauren met with the janitorial staff and told them that she expected the place to be clean and free of offensive odor at all times. One person would be assigned to bathe the dogs regularly and keep the grounds, as well as prepare a garden spot where residents can putter with flowers and vegetables. Even janitorial staff will begin to cater to the needs of the patients. "No one will be allowed to ignore the needs of a resident," she insisted.

In a matter of weeks, the entire building was repainted in bright colors; the "family room" was enlarged; tables were added; comfortable sofas were strategically placed in the room; small, trained dogs were secured and allowed free reign in the family room only, and the entire population of the home took on a new attitude in the new environment. Residents were happier, and employees had a new drive to succeed. Administrators from other nursing homes in the area began calling to say, "It won't work. You won't be able to do it." But Lauren was determined to make it work. And because she was both owner and the most involved employee, with the most compassionate drive, she knew she could make it happen.

Lauren met with family members of the residents and presented the home's new philosophy and plans. She informed them that because of more expensive service, they would be expected to pay a little more but promised to make their service worth any increase. And she asked if any of them would like to be a part of an organized group of volunteers, say a "Helping Hands Club," to provide such help as they could. Several volunteered, and everyone applauded her drive to provide the best home possible for their loved ones.

Several interesting people were a part of the home's residents. Mae Parker, although 88 years of age, still played the piano like the professional she was. She had taught music at the university and played for the services at First Church until her retirement at the age of 82. She had to be assisted to the piano but once she was seated on the bench, age and health were not factors in her performance. Every day she spent some time playing, and if she didn't do so voluntarily someone was asking her to.

Jim Green was a story teller and nearly always had a group around him listening to his latest yarn. He was "Uncle Jim" to everyone. As Lauren walked by him one day, she overheard him telling about his fox-hunting grandfather. "Why my old grandpappy would rather go fox hunting than eat. He always kept ten or twelve hounds in the pen, and a couple of nights a week he loaded them in his dog crate in the back of his old pickup and took them out to one of his favorite spots and turned them loose to chase foxes. Oh, he wouldn't have killed one of them foxes for nothing; he just loved to hear the dogs howling behind them. One time when I was about twelve he allowed me to go with him one night. 'Now, boy, we may be out there most of the night,' he said, 'so I don't want you whining to come home, you hear?'

"'Yes, Sir,' I promised.

"Well, we went way out in the country on this dirt road, and some of his cronies brought their dogs and met us there, and they all turned those eager dogs aloose. Now there was a house about a quarter of a mile down that road from us, and I could hear really loud music coming from it. Once those dogs jumped a fox and took out a'ter him, all I could hear was 'yaw, yaw, yaw.' In a little bit Grandpappy spit his tobacco juice into the little campfire and said, 'Jim, that's beautiful music, ain't it?' Now he was talking about all that barking, but I didn't know that, so I answered, 'I don't know, I can't hear it for all them dogs a barking.' I didn't know why then, but everybody just busted out a laughing."

Then there was Al Koontz, everybody said he was the man with the green thumb. When he came to TLC he was the unhappiest resident there. Severely depressed, he stayed to himself and refused to join in any of the activities. One day after he had been at the home for a month, Lauren found him sitting alone, looking out the window. "Good morning, Mr. Koontz," she greeted him cheerfully.

"Yeah, what's so good about it?" he responded.

"You seem very unhappy, Sir."

"Yeah, wouldn't you be if you had been dragged out of your home and thrown into this place where you can't even smoke and do what you want?" Koontz grumbled.

"Mr. Koontz, what would you most like to do?" Lauren probed.

"Go home."

"Would you like for me to talk with your family and see if we can arrange it?" she asked.

"Could you do that?" he asked with excitement.

"Well, if you are sure that's what you want, I'll try, " Lauren promised. " We want you to be happy. You think about why you are here in the first place and how your life would be better at your home; then tomorrow we will talk about it again. Okay?"

The next day, Lauren found Mr. Koontz alone in his room. "Let's go sit on the back porch," she suggested. She led the way, and Al trudged along beside her. When they were seated in lawn chairs, she asked, " Have you thought any more about going home, Mr. Koontz?"

"Yes, I thought about it a lot but I decided that I need to stay here. I know my family thinks they are doing the best thing for me putting me here. I lost my wife three years ago, and I was living there all alone and mighty lonesome. Then I was trying to cook and let something catch the kitchen on fire. Next I decided I would just eat cereal, but I began to lose a lot of weight. My son and daughter-in-law couldn't come to see me very often for they have their own lives and jobs, and I didn't want to be a burden on them," Koontz answered.

"What would make you happy here?" Mr. Koontz.

"Well, I'd like to be able to smoke my pipe, and what I miss most is my garden," he replied.

"Your garden? What did you grow Al?" she asked.

"All kinds of vegetables and flowers."

"Hey, that's good news," Lauren said. "Do you see that broken ground over there? That is a place for residents to putter in a garden, but so far no one has used it. Would you like to be the first to grow something there?"

"Yes, I would," he perked up. "But you know I have to stop and rest a lot, so at home I have a patio table with an umbrella. Could I bring it down here and put it out there by the garden?"

"Yes, I think you could."

"One more thing, is that far enough away from the building that I could smoke my pipe out there?" Al asked.

"I believe it is. However, you must know that smoking is not good for you," Lauren scolded.

"Good, good, "Al said gleefully, ignoring her advice. "I'll get my son to bring the umbrella and my favorite lawn chair and my garden tools and get me some seeds and fertilizer this weekend. It's time to plant right now, so I'd like to begin next week."

From that day Al Koontz had a new attitude. He became friendly and loved taking people out to his garden spot. He even interested some of the other residents in joining him in the garden. He could be seen often, smoking his Sherlock Holmes style pipe as he rested in his chair in the shade of that umbrella. You could just look out of the back windows and see him puttering in the beautiful vegetable and flower gardens all the time. Some days when he couldn't be coaxed to come in for lunch, the aides took his lunch out to the garden. He was so proud of his latest blossom or fruit and always called attention to them. He would bring them into the home and show them proudly to residents and guests. When possible they were used to brighten the home. And on occasion some of the vegetables contributed to their meals.

The only "young" resident was Ray Freeman, a veteran who had lost both legs after being hit by shrapnel in Iraq. Although he didn't have the years behind him that the other residents did, he became a part of all of the activities. He would wheel his chair around the entire home, greeting people and cheering them up. He sometimes coaxed quiet, sullen patients to play a game of checkers and livened their day.

Several weeks passed during which most of the changes took place and the rumors of the improvements at TLC had circulated widely. So the home filled to capacity and there was a waiting list of people wanting to come there. Then one warm May Saturday morning Ken Phillips, the state inspector, came to TLC for a surprise visit. What he saw shocked him: fifteen to twenty family members were in the family room with their relatives. One female resident was holding a dog in her lap petting it calmly. One patient was teaching another to crochet. Four men sat at a round table playing dominoes. Six patients could be seen through the back window working in the garden. Fresh flowers adorned the family room. Classical music came from an upscale entertainment center. A few residents dozed, but no one was crying out for attention or seemed disgruntled.

The first person to greet Phillips was the story teller, Jim Green. "Hello, young fella, he called out. I'm Jim. Where you from?"

"I'm from Baton Rouge," he responded politely.

"Let me tell you about the time I met Governor Long," Jim began his tale. "Yes, Sir. I went to Baton Rouge to talk to him. I was there in front of the state capital building when I seen him coming with three or four body guards around him. 'Hey, Earl,' I called out. His body guards tried to keep me away from him, but he just turned and said, 'Hey, yourself. Who are you?' Well, I told him my name and that I had come to see him about some important matters. Then he said, 'Well, let's go inside and find a comfortable place to sit and smoke a cigar.' So he took me into his big office and we talked for a while. 'Governor,' I says. 'Our roads are in a mess and we need to do something about them. And we got a lot of poor people who need help, so I'm asking you to do something about it.'

"'By George, I'm glad you told me, Jim,' he said, ' and I promise you I'm going to fix the problems.' And I tell you he did it too. He was a good man. They run him crazy though. Wound up in the nut house before he died."

"Will you excuse me?" Phillips asked. "I need to speak with Mrs. Jenson."

"Who are all of these people here?" he demanded of Lauren.

"Oh, they are family members who've come to be a part of their relatives' lives."

"You must have found out some way that I was making this surprise visit and set this up to make your institution look good," he accused Lauren.

"This isn't an institution, Mr. Griffin," Lauren insisted; " it's a home for seniors who have families who care about them and want the best for them. You can see that the loved ones are here today, as they often are, to visit and to participate with their family members. They have formed a 'Helping Hands Club,' and you can see some of them here all the time."

"I see." Unconvinced, Phillips asked, " I wonder if you would object to my meeting with these family members."

"Certainly not," Lauren responded." Just go into the chapel and I'll round them up and bring them in to you."

When eighteen family members, who were all a part of the "Helping Hands Club," were assembled in the chapel, Lauren introduced Mr. Griffin and told them his business. "He would like to meet with you, so I'm going to go about my job to allow you some privacy with him."

When Lauren was out of the room, Griffin said, "This isn't real. I visit nursing homes all over the state and I've never seen anything like it. It has to be a setup to make the place look good. Tell me what your major complaints are, and don't hold anything back. I want to hear you biggest gripes."

No one spoke, so after a few minutes, Griffin urged them, "C'mon folks, don't you have something to say?"

"We do, Mr. Griffin," one lady spoke up. "But you asked for complaints and we don't have any gripes about TLC. Our biggest complaint is that when a caring, innovative person, like Lauren, comes in here and makes this a model home, you feel compelled to come here and try to find fault with it. My mother has been in two other places that were state-approved 'institutions,' but we never had the atmosphere or the service that we are getting here. We are having to pay a little more now, but for the better care my mother is getting, I'm glad to do it."

Another lady spoke up and said, "Mr. Griffin, if you want to write up a report, write about the excessive state and government regulations that restrict and hamper the well being of our loved ones. Let's go folks." With that, they marched back to the family room and Mr. Griffin took his brief case and departed out the side door without seeing Lauren again.

CHAPTER 5

Two busy years had passed since Benji's birth and Lauren and Rusty had not yet been blessed with a little brother or sister for him. They had hoped and prayed for one for some time but had seen no results; then Lauren began noticing some telltale signs. Although she didn't want to tell anyone until she was sure, she paid close attention to the early morning nausea and other symptoms she was all too familiar with. A month later the doctor confirmed what she already knew; then she broke the news to the rest of the family. Rusty was ecstatic and even Benji began to anticipate a little brother or sister. Marie urged her daughter to slow down, "You've been working too hard for two years now. You have to get more rest and take care of yourself. Your competent staff can take care of TLC if you will let them."

"I know, Mom. I'll try," Lauren promised. So she and Rusty decided to take a week's vacation in the mountains. Despite Marie's objections they couldn't go off and leave Benji and Marie at home, so they all went to the Ozarks where they rented a cabin in a private, but scenic area. They rested, walked the hiking trails and sat on the porch and watched the beautiful sunsets every evening. However, neither of them could relax fully for thinking of the businesses at home and what they needed to be there doing.

However, as much as they wanted another child, it was not to be, for three months into the pregnancy, Lauren began to cramp and Rusty rushed her to the hospital, but the next morning the doctor informed them that she had lost the baby. Marie blamed it on her daughter's overwork. Rusty and Lauren grieved the loss and wondered why God would let them get their hopes up and then allow this to happen. Bitter at first, they soon came to accept their loss and say, "God knows what He is doing. When He wants us to have another baby He will provide it, and until then we will just enjoy the one we have."

One evening Rusty sat on the back porch and watched Benji play in the yard. Pointing to a little three-inch oak bush, Benji asked, "What 'dis?"

"Well, Son," Rusty explained, "that's a baby tree from this mother tree."

The child wandered from under the shelter of the tree and pointed to the ground and said, "No baby."

"That's right, son. You see when the acorns fall from a tree they don't fall far from it. Then when those acorns sprout they give life to a new tree just like the tree the acorn came from. I know you won't understand this yet, but it's like a baby that comes from his parents and takes on the characteristics of his mom and dad. That's why we say that the acorn never falls far from the tree."

"Uh huh." But by then Benji was interested in a worm.

Meanwhile far to the south, in the Crescent City, a budding young corporate attorney was beginning to make his mark. A year earlier he had graduated from the state's largest law school with honors and joined a prestigious law firm whose partners boasted forty years of practice and success. Vincent Grimillion was a conscientious, by-the-book thirty something year old. Like many in his generation, he exercised daily, ate healthy, and lived with his girlfriend. Most mornings he began his day with a jog in the New Orleans City Park, a sprawling 13,000-acre picturesque showplace which boasted the world's largest stand of live oak trees. Its history dates back to 1854, making it one of the nation's oldest urban parks. During the Great Depression and following it, Roosevelt's Works Progress Administration (WPA) spent $12 million on the site making it the envy of the South. It was just one of the 1,410,000 projects including, roads, bridges, public buildings and airport landing fields completed by the 3,400,000 participants between 1935 and 1943.

On a balmy Friday morning, Vincent rose before daylight, and leaving Nicole asleep, he slipped out of the apartment and went for his morning run. He had made his normal route under a canopy of moss-covered oak trees and had slowed to a walk to catch his breath as he cooled down. Morning light was breaking the horizon so he had no difficulty seeing and was paying little attention to his surroundings until he heard a faint cry. At first he thought it might be the meow of a cat, but listening closely he discovered that it was more, human perhaps, a baby maybe. He turned aside to a park bench on which there was a cardboard box and got the surprise of his life when he looked inside into the face of a newborn baby which had been carefully wrapped in a blanket. Looking all around for some adult who might have carelessly left her baby there, in the distance he caught just a glimpse of someone peeking around the trunk of a tree. "Hey," he yelled. "Is this your baby?" When she disappeared, he ran a few yards after her before she lost herself among the trees.

What should he do? He couldn't leave this infant exposed to who knows what. To call the police seemed like a heartless thing to do. He might have asked someone else what to do, but no one was in sight at the early hour. "I guess I'll have to take you home, little one," he spoke aloud. Nicole will know what to do." So he carefully lifted the box with its precious cargo, and headed out for his apartment a few blocks away. At the apartment, he slipped his key into the lock and opened the door to find Nicole still asleep. When he put the box on the coffee table, however, the infant let out a wail that brought Nicole running to investigate. She almost fainted when she looked into the box and demanded loudly, "Where did you get this baby?" Vincent told her the story and confessed that he didn't know what to do and that he thought she would know.

"How should I know?" she questioned. "I don't know anything about babies, except I know we will need to find some milk for it." With that she lifted the baby from the box and cradled it in her arms as if it belonged there. "Is it a boy or a girl?" she asked as she began removing the blanket. Inside she found a newborn girl without any clothing under the blanket. "She hasn't even been cleaned up since birth. Get some warm water and a soft wash cloth, Vincent, and let's clean her little body. Then we have to decide what to do with her. Then run down to that twenty-four-hour pharmacy and get a baby bottle and some diapers." Vincent grabbed his wallet and, still in his jogging clothes, ran for the pharmacy. In no time he was back with two baby bottles, two pacifiers, two boxes of diapers, and some baby blankets. He found Nicole cooing to a clean, sweet-smelling baby wrapped in a soft towel.

"What are we going to do with her?" Vincent asked.

" Where did you find her? Do you think someone will come for her? Did anyone watch you take her? What if you are accused of kidnapping?" Questions flowed from Nicole.

"I don't know anything about her. I'm sure no one saw me except for the woman who ran away. Maybe she is the mother."

"Can we keep her, Vincent?" Nicole asked.

"Oh, no. I don't think so. I mean I love babies, but I'm sure we need to report this to the authorities."

"Well, let's wait a little while. I'm out of school now, so I can care for her until we find out what to do. First, I need to take her to a doctor today to have her checked out," Nicole suggested.

"You can't take her in the car without a car seat, so as soon as I'm ready for work I'll go buy one."

At 9:00 Nicole began calling pediatricians for an early appointment. The earliest she could get was across town at 11:00, so she began getting herself and the baby ready. At 10:45 she eased her Lexus into the last space at the office, removed the baby from the carrier, and carried the infant inside the office in her arms. Once inside Nicole was asked to fill out multiple sheets of questions she couldn't answer, such as name, date of birth, parents' names, allergies, medical history. Exasperated, she finally asked, "May I just see the doctor, please?"

When she was in the doctor's examining room, a young female soon entered and introduced herself, "Good morning. I'm doctor Craft. How may I help you today?" Nicole had to tell the story of Vincent finding the baby and the circumstances and that she wanted the doctor to examine the infant. "We don't really know what to do," she confessed.

After examining the baby and declaring her healthy, the doctor excused herself, promising to return shortly. Half an hour later she returned and informed Nicole, "I'm sorry, but I've had to call the police. You see, a female infant was stolen from the hospital last night, and I'm required by law to report this."

"I understand," Nicole responded. "Maybe the woman who left her in the park had taken her. We just didn't know what to do." It never crossed her mind that she and Vincent might be suspects.

But when Doctor Craft took the baby and opened the door, two policemen were standing in the little hallway. "M'am I regret to inform you

Falling Acorns

that you are under arrest for suspicion of kidnapping. Turn around please," they ordered Nicole. For the first time in her life she felt the handcuffs snap around her wrists. "Come with us please."

"Wait, let me call Vincent," Nicole said.

"You can call him later," they assured her. In the patrol car she would have secretly used her cell phone if she could have reached it but her hands were cuffed behind her and the phone was in her purse. At the police station, Nicole was escorted in like a common criminal. It was so humiliating. She was ushered into a small room with faded blue walls and seated at a scarred table. She wondered how many other innocent victims had sat at this old table and been drilled for answers.

"May I call Vincent now?" Nicole begged, beginning to cry. "I've done nothing wrong, I tell you. I have just been taking care of the baby until we could report finding her."

"Okay, but we just need to ask you a few questions," the officer explained. "Tell us how you came to have this newborn baby." Nicole told the story of Vincent finding the infant in the park, bringing her home, and how they cared for her until they could decide what action to take.

"How long have you had the baby?" the policeman asked again.

"Since 6:00 this morning."

"Why didn't you call the police earlier?" he wanted to know.

"Look, my fiancée is an attorney, but we just didn't know what to do. Call him. He will explain," she pleaded.

"We will let you call him soon."

The policeman left her alone for a while, then returned to grill her some more and have her repeat the story. Finally, upon returning, he said, "All right, Ma'm. You may call you husband now."

"He's my boyfriend," she explained as she began dialing the phone. When Vincent came on the phone, she burst into tears and blurted out, "Vincent, you have to hurry to the police station."

"What's wrong?" he asked.

"I'm being held on suspicion of kidnapping. I'll explain it when you get here, just hurry."

"Okay, I'm on my way," Vincent promised.

Ten minutes later he entered the station where an officer approached him and asked, "Are you Vincent Gremillion?"

"Yes, I'm looking for Nicole Thibodeaux," he replied.

"You'll have to come with me," the officer explained. Taken to an empty room, Vincent was questioned extensively about the baby and how he came to have her in his possession. He understood that they were gathering information from both him and Nicole to corroborate their stories.

"Where is the baby?" he asked.

"The Department of Children and Family Services (DCFS) is taking care of her. She is being checked out at the hospital right now."

"May I see Nicole?"

"In due time," they promised, and left him alone.

A half an hour later, a smiling officer opened the door with Nicole at his side. "I have good news," he said. "The hospital has compared this baby's footprint with the one that was kidnapped and they do not match. So you are free to go."

Nicole fell into Vincent's arms, crying. "When can we get the baby back," Vincent asked.

"I'm afraid that's impossible for now. The baby is in the custody of DCFS who will be investigating and trying to find the mother," the officer explained.

"Will we be able to get her back later?" Nicole asked.

"I guess that will be up to them, but you may call them and inquire if you like. They should be able to tell you what to expect. Good luck. You're free to go now. I'm sorry for the inconvenience" he apologized.

The next morning Vincent called DCFS to inquire about the baby and to request that he and Nicole be granted custody of the infant and to eventually adopt her. "We can't make you any promises except that your request will be noted, but we can tell you that a hearing will be conducted next week to determine the future of the child," the worker informed him. Immediately, Vincent and Nicole began preparing their case to request the baby. The hearing was to be held before Judge Julian Arceneaux Tuesday morning at 9:00.

Vincent and Nicole were there early. And when the hearing began, Vincent made his case and requested that the baby be assigned to them. Then the DCFS official followed with a brief discussion of the failure of the investigation to discover any information about the child's mother. "Our recommendation, Your Honor, is that the request of Vincent Gremillion and Nicole Thibodeaux be denied because they are not married. And second, that the baby be placed with a family far away from New Orleans so the natural mother will have no possibility of knowing where the baby is or of contacting the adopting family."

"We will have a fifteen minute recess after which I'll return with my decision," the judge announced. When court re-convened, the judge spoke directly to Vincent and Nicole: "I appreciate the care you have given to the foundling and your willingness to adopt her. However, I am denying your request because you are not married. Since you are unwilling to commit to each other in a permanent relationship, I question your willingness to make such a commitment to this stranger. If you are so eager to have a child, I suggest that you marry and produce a legitimate child of your own. Furthermore, I approve the recommendation to place this baby with a family somewhere in north Louisiana, which I think will be better for all concerned."

On their way home, Vincent grieved over the court's decision and voiced his regret to Nicole. But when she spoke up, she said, "Vincent, I haven't said anything before, but I had some serious reservations about taking the baby. I don't think I'm ready for a baby, especially someone else's. And I agree with the judge that if we want to start a family we should begin with marriage." Vincent knew she was right and began formulating a plan in his mind to propose to Nicole soon. He would begin immediately to shop for a ring and reserve a place in some romantic setting to propose properly.

CHAPTER 6

Lauren was back in church three weeks later when a social worker friend, employed by DCFS, approached her and asked if she could call on her at TLC the next morning. Lauren agreed, thinking that it had something to do with elder care. At 9:00, Monday morning Mary Fellows came into Lauren's office and broke the news to her, "I have a newborn girl who needs a home immediately."

"Mary, I cannot take a foster child and risk having to give her up in a few months," Lauren answered.

"I understand," Mary replied. "But this baby is available for immediate adoption. If you agree, she will be in your care until all the investigation and paper work are done; then a judge will grant you the right to adopt."

"Where is this baby from?" Lauren wanted to know.

"A jogger in New Orleans found her in a cardboard box on a park bench. He took her home and then she wound up in our New Orleans office and they arranged for her temporary care. Now we want to put her in a home where she can be adopted in short order. You see, the only thing we know about her is her date of birth, based on when she was found, obviously newborn. No mother's name. No name for the baby. No address. She was not born in a hospital. We tried to find the mother with no success. So we have moved her away from where her mother probably is so she can never interfere in her life or yours."

"How soon will she be available?" Lauren asked.

"This afternoon," Mary answered. " And I'll need your answer soon. Please understand that I'm not trying to push this on you, but I know that you want another baby and that you've just lost one, so I thought of you first. What do you think?"

"I think I need to talk with Rusty and God. Can you give me until this afternoon?" Lauren asked.

Mary handed her a business card and said, "Yes. Call me as soon as you have an answer."

When Mary left, Lauren called Rusty and asked if he could get away from work and meet her at home as soon as possible.

"Sure. What wrong?" he wanted to know.

"Maybe nothing, but we have to have a family conference now."

Bewildered, Rusty rushed home to find Lauren, Marie, and Benji at the breakfast table. "What's up?" he asked. Then Lauren told them the story and asked if they could make this a family decision. Everyone was silent for a full minute.

Rusty broke the silence; "Well, let's ask God first," and he began the short prayer. Lauren followed. Marie said it was not her decision to make but that she would welcome the chance to take care of another little one.

"Benji, would you like a baby sister?" Lauren asked. His eyes lit up with excitement and he said, "I want a brudder."

"Well, I'm sorry, but this will be a sister. Will that be okay?" Lauren asked.

"I guess," he responded.

"Then it's unanimous," Rusty said. "Call her."

"Mom, can you get together some things we will need for a baby girl?" Lauren requested. That afternoon everyone came home early and Mary Fellows brought the baby. After signing the papers, Mary told them what they could expect during the adoption process; they would be checked out to be sure theirs was a suitable home, but they would surely qualify. Then they would go before a judge who, with the DCFS recommendation, would grant them custody of the child. Mary left them, a happy family, gathered around the prettiest little girl with a head full of dark hair. Everyone, even Benji, waited his or her turn to hold her carefully.

After they had passed the adorable baby around for everyone to hold, Lauren said, "I understand now why God let us lose our baby. I would not have been willing to take this one otherwise. He did know best, as He always does." After their dinner Bible reading, they thanked God for this gift of a baby girl, who was still known as Jane Doe, so they had to give her a name. Benji wanted to name her "Baby sister," but after much discussion they settled on Katherine, after her aunt Cathy.

Katherine and Benji bonded quickly and grew to become as close as any brother and sister could possibly be. Lauren and Rusty knew their children were special, at least to them, but they grew up as normal as any children could. Benji came to dote on his little sister; she became his playmate, and he assumed the role of her big brother protector. When he reached the age to enter pre-k, she cried to go with him and moped around all day until he came home. When he moved up to kindergarten and began learning new things, he brought them home and tried to teach them to Katherine.

Marie was their adult chauffeur, tutor, disciplinarian, coach, cook, and friend. She drove them to and from school every day and saw that they completed any homework assignments they had before television and play time. She loved them dearly and they reciprocated, but she could be firm with them too, demanding proper behavior and to accept responsibility.

As the siblings grew they became involved in the normal children's activities. Benji played T-ball, then Little League, and Katherine took piano lessons and played soccer.

Their parents were always very supportive. The children could count on Mom and Dad being at every ball game and piano recital, cheering them on. Even when their efforts showed little success, the parents complimented and encouraged them.

Benji's Little League coach was a godly man who believed that he should teach his team members and, therefore, had prayer with them before every game. At first he prayed; then one day he asked if one of them could lead the prayer, and all of the players pointed at Benji. From that first prayer, Benji became the chaplain of a sort and prayed all of the prayers. Not all of the boys were from active Christian homes, but they all respected Benji's devotion.

As they aged, both the children changed in their interests and activities. Benji realized that he wasn't very athletic, so he opted to play the trumpet in the school band, and be manager of the ball team. Katherine broadened her interests and became a member of every club and group for which she qualified. That meant that she was to become a model for the other girls, the helper for the teacher, and the peacemaker among the students.

When they were ten and twelve years of age, after their Bible reading from John's Gospel, chapter 3, Rusty brought up the subject of how to become a Christian. Despite their knowledge of the subject, neither of the children had made a public profession of faith. But their discussions showed that they understood God's plan for our salvation. In fact, Katherine shared with them that she had already asked Jesus to come into her heart and save her. Benji clearly understood and said that he wanted to make that decision too, so there at the dinner table Benji prayed to receive Christ and Katherine thanked the Lord for her salvation. After hugs all around, Rusty said, "I want you to know how proud I am of you. You are good children and you are Christians. Next, you need to respond to the pastor's invitation and share with him and the church your conversion experience; then you will be baptized into the fellowship of the church."

The next Sunday, Benji and Katherine were escorted to the altar by Rusty with tears streaming down his cheeks to allow them to tell Pastor Williams of their experience and desire to be baptized. He expressed gratitude for their commitment and, for the sake of the congregation, chose to question them and have them explain how one is saved. He knew they would have the correct answers and they didn't disappoint him nor their godly parents. It was hard for those who had watched their lives develop and knew that they were such good children to realize they had ever been lost.

Like most children, when they entered the teen years, they exhibited some rebellious independence, but they were always invited to talk with their parents and know that their opinions were respected. They wanted to go to teen parties, but learned that their parents would be very selective when granting them permission. When Benji was fourteen he wanted to take a girl classmate to a Saturday afternoon movie, so Marie drove them to the movie and to get pizza afterward.

Benji's bicycle became a bone of contention; he wanted to exercise his independence by riding wherever he chose, but soon realized that he was limited to only the safest places and always near home. With his friend Rick he fished in a nearby pond and loved the sport, but even more he liked the freedom to do it. He was so proud when he could bring home fish to show, then clean and cook for supper.

Katherine was so busy with all of her activities that she had little time or interest in boys. They were friends, but little more. Rusty and Lauren enjoyed the period because they knew there would come a time when they would worry when she was dating. However, she was a model daughter. Marie taught her to cook simple meals, to sew a little, and to clean house. She was trained to be a lady in all circumstances.

The Jenson family was a happy, close knit group. They did activities together, went to church together, read the Bible together, and prayed together. They were comfortable discussing their work, school, and problems together. Of course they weren't perfect; Benji had a quick temper and a streak of independence, and Katherine was known to pout at times until she got her way. But they never disobeyed their parents or engaged in any misbehavior. Rusty remembered the words of that country western song, "Why Me, Lord," and asked himself why he could be so blessed. Oh, he was grateful, but he saw so many other good, God-fearing people, suffering major illnesses, having family problems, and drug addiction among the teenagers and wondered why he had been so blessed.

Benji and Katherine's parents and Grandmother Marie had taught them well and they had grown to be responsible, at home and elsewhere. They kept their rooms clean, helped with the dishes after each meal and with other household chores.

CHAPTER 7

The halfway houses were ready for occupancy. Rusty had employed a contractor to come in and re-design some of the rooms so that there were now a commons room, double- occupancy bedrooms, a kitchen and three bathrooms. Some of the neighbors were apprehensive about having ex-convicts as neighbors and expressed their concerns to Rusty, but he assured them that these men and women were so happy to get out of jail that they would cause no trouble because of the risk of being sent back. However, he assured them that any problem residents would be moved out immediately. He had found two women to manage the houses and cook the meals for the residents, and they began immediately following Rusty's program for worship, Bible study, and Wednesday night group sessions.

When Rusty learned that some women would be coming too, he decided to use the smaller house for them and Clark's home for the men. Knowing from personal experience that successful rehabilitation requires a change of heart, he planned for the homes to be Christ centered. Bible studies were scheduled regularly, and transportation was provided for them to go to Sunday services at local churches if they wished to go. Strict rules as outlined by the Department of Corrections were enforced. Alcohol or drug use or the refusal to work at an outside job meant a trip back to jail. Disputes were settled in a manner that befitted mature adults. Every Wednesday evening Rusty had group sessions where he provided experienced guidance. The Corrections officers said that his homes became models for others because Rusty made them rehabilitation centers not just a lesser form of incarceration.

All good things will be challenged, however, and it was no different at the halfway houses. Fights broke out and drastic measures had to be enforced. Alcohol was smuggled in and had to be stopped immediately. It didn't take long for one newcomer to object to the religious activities and to contact the ACLU about them. The notice arrived in a registered letter, informing Rusty that he was being sued to cease and desist imposing his religious beliefs on the residents. He simply took the notice to his attorney who pledged to do all within his power to settle the matter. But, despite his best efforts, the ACLU refused to budge. They wanted nothing less than an appearance in court and the publicity that would come with it.. Meanwhile, Rusty continued the studies and told the residents to attend or go back to prison. Grudgingly the challenger continued to attend, but in every session he raised skeptical questions and argued about the answers. Then at one Wednesday night meeting, he challenged Rusty, "What makes you think you know so much about it, anyway?" Since he had opened wide the door, Rusty had the opportunity to share his own story. He tried to get them to see and admit, at least to themselves, responsibility for their actions. Most of them blamed their problems on someone else, refusing to admit responsibility, but Rusty taught them that the first step in rehabilitation is to accept one's own responsibility. "Stop blaming others; be honest with yourself; admit your guilt," he insisted. "Then you can deal with it."

Rusty had turned the matter over to Attorney Albertson, so he continued his normal routine, but ACLU's goal was to call attention to Rusty's program and try to stop it. Court appearances, and negotiations lasted for months until the final court decision. Judge Adams, a firm, but level headed judge, presided over the case. The ACLU attorney took a full day to present his case, citing precedents, and freedom of religion issues. When Rusty's attorney presented the defense he had the statistics showing the early success of the program. He granted the request from some of the residents that they be allowed to testify to the effectiveness of the program. After a morning of defense, a noon recess was called and the judge promised a decision after lunch.

When the court reconvened at 1:30 Judge Adams addressed the plaintiff and Attorney Winegarten. "Mr. Winegarten, why is it that whenever someone tries to do something good for others in particular and society in general you and the ACLU find fault and try to stop it. You claim it is because it violates the principle of freedom of religion, but I'll tell you that I'm convinced that what Mr. Jenson is doing is far better for society than what you and your cohorts advocate. Understand that the opportunity to be in a halfway house is a privilege not an obligation, so anyone who objects to the program there may return to the prison at any time upon his or her request. Religious instruction and personal evangelism are being conducted at Angola State Prison also and it has proven to reduce the violence tremendously and enhance rehabilitation. I cannot understand why a man who is offered the opportunity to better himself and be prepared to re-enter mainstream society would object. I think this is a frivolous suit without merit and I'm ruling in favor of the defense. Now, Mr. Winegarten, I do not wish to see you back in my courtroom ever again. Do you understand?"

"Yes, your Honor."

The plaintiff stood and asked, "May I say something your Honor?'

"You may if it's not a challenge to the court's decision," the judge answered.

"No, Sir, it isn't. Since I initiated this action, I've had a change of heart because I've seen the good that the program is doing. It has helped me too. In fact, I tried to stop this suit, but Mr. Winegarten said I had to go through with it, so he proceeded over my objections. I apologize to Mr. Jenson and to the court, Your Honor."

"Shame on you, Mr. Winegarten!" Judge Adams scolded. " Court is adjourned."

Rusty knew that the program had to be Christ centered. He would not have continued it otherwise. Some of the folks at First Church were not too happy to see him bringing ten to fifteen African Americans, Caucasians, and Mexicans from the halfway houses to fill two pews on Sunday morning, but he was convinced that was the way God wanted it, and if God approved he didn't worry too much about others.

Many good results came from Rusty's efforts in that ministry. When the time came for one of the home's residents to be discharged they all made it a celebratory event. It was like a commencement party with a special meal. The inmate's family was invited and Rusty had arranged for some certificates that indicated that a person had completed the rehabilitation program. On occasion, those who remained in the area were asked to return to speak to those still in the program, reporting on their lives since they had moved back into main society. They told of how the public treated them, the challenges they faced, and their successes. Those with positive results were an inspiration to others who would come after them. A few of the discharged wanted to come back every Wednesday evening to the group sessions, but space was limited so only a few were allowed.

Even though the men and women were completely separated, they came together for the "graduation" ceremonies, and out of that contact some lasting relationships and even marriages developed. An African American couple married as soon as they were released, and the lady who cooked and ran the house for the men fell in love with a man who often helped her in the kitchen. Because the rules prohibited an open romantic relationship, they courted very discreetly and announced at his release that they would be married. She continued to work there and he worked at Clark's Woodworking.

The Department of Corrections noted the success of Rusty's program and in a public recognition ceremony the governor came and presented him with an Award of Excellence. As a result, Rusty was approved as a consultant to other halfway houses around the state, so he frequently traveled to advise those who were just beginning or those who were having trouble.

State Corrections required that the residents had to give up part of the wages they earned to contribute to their care. In addition, those who saw the good that was being accomplished, such as family members, and friends, contributed to the operation of the homes. Those sources of income added to the generous amount accumulating in the Eva Howie Foundation meant that the program was on solid ground financially. So Rusty began dreaming of expanding the program to include more inmate residences.

Chapter 8

With sound management and skilled craftsmanship Clark's Woodworking was doing well. A good relationship was enjoyed among all of the men and the lady who had been hired as secretary. However, Rusty was always looking for opportunities to improve and expand the business. So when the local building store owner approached him with the idea of opening a door and window shop he was interested. "I've talked with the other building supply store owners in the area, but none of us feel that we want to take on the business ourselves. Since you have the space and the know-how, Rusty, if you will build a shop to manufacture wooden doors and windows we will all order ours from you." After a thorough investigation, Rusty saw it as a possibility, so he began to make plans to build an additional shop and train workmen to staff it.

The first step was at the attorney's office to enlist his help. He advised Rusty to create a separate business. "You know this will be a separate business, so you will not need to share your profits from it with the Eva Howie Foundation," he offered. Rusty had not considered that so it had not been a factor in his decision to start the business. When the paper work was done, he enlisted a builder to erect a building large enough to house the equipment, supplies, and provide storage. Then he shopped for and purchased the specialized equipment he would need in the shop.

The expansion required hiring additional skilled craftsmen, so Rusty was able to move Joe, one of the most capable men from the woodworking shop, to be in charge of the new business. And because he was always trying to help the residents of the halfway house he gave one of them the chance to learn the trade and replace Joe in the original shop; then one man and a woman were enlisted to start learning the work of building doors and windows in the new shop.

Benji loved his father and begged to go to the shop with him. Rusty would not allow it when work was being done but took him on Saturdays when he needed to go do some clean up or office work. Finally, when Benji reached twelve, Rusty gave him a job away from the machinery after school. He loved it and couldn't wait until he was old enough to run the saws and other machinery and assemble the pieces into finished products. In the summers Benji began staying at the shop all day, every day. And so it went until he reached sixteen. By then, Rusty had trained him to respect the machinery and to use it safely. He was careful and reliable, so Rusty rewarded him by buying a new Jeep for him to drive. He was allowed to drive it to school and to work, but parental permission was required to go elsewhere.

There is a saying that every teenager has to climb fool's hill at some point, and Benji's climb began when he was seventeen. He was beginning to date and some of the girls were having too much influence on his life. Jane Williams seemed to have the most affect; she tried to persuade Benji to try drugs and alcohol, assuring him that all young people were doing it and that there was no harm in it. He refused until she coaxed him to go to a teen party at a friend's house. "It'll be fun," she insisted. However, his convictions were about to be tested as never before. When he and Jane arrived he discovered that there were about a dozen older teens already there, but no adults. He would learn that the parents were away on a trip and the young people had free reign. Soon a keg of beer was tapped and the contents spread around. Benji had never tasted the drink and planned to refuse now. He had been genuinely saved five years earlier and had steadfastly stuck to Christian principles since. However, the pressure was on; "You have to try it, Benji," urged Jane. "Just a little bit won't hurt you." All of the others joined in saying, "You are here with us, so you have to participate. We can't have you going off to tell others what we did here."

Benji accepted the glass of beer and planned to just sip it, but after one he didn't think that it had affected him, so he decided to try another one. After all, he thought, my dad used to do it. Before long marijuana was being passed around and the beer had lowered his inhibitions enough that he decided, "why not?" The others were so pleased that they gave him their full attention to see how he would react. Soon he was in a state of oblivion and accepting everything that was handed to him. Others were pairing up and moving to other rooms in the house, and then Jane said, "Come on, it's our turn in the bedroom." Blindly, he followed her lead and the next thing he remembered was waking up without any clothes on and Jane was no where in sight. Quickly he dressed and searched the house. Everyone else was either passed out or sleeping soundly. He shook Jane to say, "Come on, we have to go." But she refused; "Not now," she said with slurred speech. Regardless of how much he tried, he couldn't persuade her to leave, so he made his way to the Jeep and left without her and drove home erratically.

The experience was so out of character for Benji that he thought he would never do it again, but he was so ashamed and filled with guilt that he tried to shake it by continuing to experiment with drink and drugs. Jane always knew where the parties were being held and persuaded him to go with her for repeat performances. Not only was he introduced to alcohol and marijuana, but he was soon getting injections of something they said was "harmless."

Rusty and Lauren were convinced that Benji had received the Lord, so they were surprised when he began to show some serious changes in personality and behavior. Finally he had yielded to the temptations and found that he really enjoyed the lifestyle of so many other young people. So drinking and drugs became a regular habit for him. At home he became withdrawn and defensive when his parents tried to talk to him about it. They prayed for him and with him and warned him about the dangers to which he was being exposed.

Benji's school work began to slide, so it didn't take him long to decide that he didn't need school. Even though his parents objected vehemently, he refused to attend classes. After all, he argued, he was always going to work in the woodworking shop and nothing he was learning in school was going to help him. His father's teaching and experience were all he would need, he insisted. Failing to keep him in school, Rusty insisted that he would have to go to work fulltime and gave him a job in the shop. But Benji's work habits declined also. He made careless and costly mistakes, came in to work late almost every day, and accomplished little in the shop. When Rusty talked with him about it, he argued that he was an adult and he would do as he pleased. He never had any money, so his parents feared that he had fallen into some costly addiction. Finally, he announced that he was quitting his job.

Rusty and Lauren knew that it was time to take painful action, so they scheduled a family meeting to deal with the problem. Benji didn't show up for it, so they planned another one when they knew he would be home. Rusty went into Benji's room as he slept, smelling of alcohol and marijuana, and took the keys to the Jeep. But when Benji discovered they were about to have a meeting, he said, "You all go ahead. I'm out of here. I don't have to put up with any more lectures." However, when he couldn't find the keys, he was trapped for he wasn't about to walk anywhere. Rusty and Lauren just listened as he raved about them taking away all his freedom.

Rusty, Lauren, Marie, and Kathrine sat around the table with Benji. "Son," Rusty began, "first I want you to know that we all love you. In fact, we love you so much that we cannot allow you to live in this house the way you are living without taking some action. We watched you grandfather pet and pamper your mom's brother Ben and allow him free reign, and you know where it got him. We love you too much to help you live the way you are. We believe that you are a Christian, but you have drifted far from God and His way. You say you are an adult and free to do as you please, so we are going to help you to be independent. We are going to rent you an apartment and pay the first month's rent and give you $100, and we will help you move out of our home and into the apartment. You will not be allowed to eat your meals here except for Sunday lunch with us after you go to church. You cannot do your laundry here, nor hang out here."

"You mean you're kicking me out?" Benji asked.

"No, you are choosing to leave and we are allowing it. You see if you live here you have to abide by our rules and practice Christian standards. Apparently that isn't what you have chosen to do now," Rusty informed him.

"I guess I'll have to come back to work at that stupid shop," Benji complained.

"No, Benji, you don't have a job there anymore," Rusty said. "You remember you quit."

"You mean you won't hire me back?" Benji asked.

"That's right. Since you want to be free from our ways and rules, you will need to work for someone else. With your experience. there may be another shop in town that will hire you, but you will have to find your own job. Son, I want you to know that we love you and anytime you are willing to come home physically and spiritually you may, but not until you make those changes. I hope you will read the story of the prodigal son in Luke 15 and see that it is your story. For now, why don't you get your things together and I'll drive you to the apartment."

"Naw, I'll just take my Jeep."

"I'm sorry to inform you," Rusty said, "but you don't have a Jeep."

"What?" Benji shouted. "Do you mean you are taking my Jeep away from me too?"

"No. If you check, you will see that it's my Jeep. It's in my name, I paid for it, and I pay the insurance. I can't have you driving my vehicle when you are high on drugs or have been drinking. You know, Benji, I've been down the road you are on and you see what it cost me. I don't want that to happen to you," Rusty responded.

"But how will I get around or get to work when I find a job?"

"I guess you'll have to walk. When I first went to work for Clark, I walked three miles to work. After what I had been through, I didn't mind at all. It was much easier than marching out to the fields and working all day at Angola, then having to walk back."

"I just can't believe you are doing this to me," Benji complained.

"No, son, we are not doing this to you; you are doing it to yourself," Rusty responded. "If this is the kind of lifestyle you choose, you will have to manage it. I will no longer enable you to live like you are. Now, if you see the error of your ways and come back repentant and changed, you will be welcomed back. Don't forget that. When you are ready, the first step will be to leave the friends who are influencing you and make new ones. But you must remember that even though they are influencing you, no one but you is responsible for your actions."

"Is that all of this 'meeting?'" Benji demanded.

"Yes, you may go gather your things."

Angrily, Benji threw his clothes and electronics in boxes and hauled them out to Rusty's truck. Lauren and Katerine said tearful goodbyes and Rusty drove him to the rented apartment and helped him to carry everything inside. Then he forced Benji to allow him to hug him and say again, "Anytime you are ready to abide by our conditions, go back to school, work part time, give up drugs and alcohol you will be welcome at home. And if you need help to make those changes, we will get it for you." Then Rusty walked away with tears streaming down his cheeks.

CHAPTER 9

When Benji had blown off his steam and cooled down a bit, he put his things away in the apartment and began looking around. The electricity and the water were on, but when he tried to call his girlfriend, he discovered there was no phone service and no television. He looked in the refrigerator and found it empty, as was the pantry. "I guess I'll have to spend the $100 getting something in here to eat," he grumbled. "Then what?" He walked to the nearest grocery store where he bought milk, bread, sandwich meat, and soft drinks and carried them home. He counted his money and found that he had only $70 left. When night came, Benji walked to the hangout where his friends would be and lied and told them his Jeep was broke down. He also told them about his new pad and invited them over. After a couple of hours at the hangout, they loaded into three cars and drove to the apartment.

"Hey, where's the beer?" they asked. "Do you have any weed stashed here?' When they discovered Benji had nothing to party with and little money to buy anything, they decided to hang out some other place. Even Jane left with the group, leaving Benji all alone. The next day he hitched a ride to the nearest woodworking shop but they refused to hire him.

Then he went to the only other sizeable shop in town, where the owner, Bill Johnson, was a friend of Rusty's. Benji had no idea that his dad had called Bill and told him the situation and asked if he would give Benji a job if he came asking for it, and Bill agreed to try him.

"You say you are Rusty Jenson's son?" Johnson asked.

"Yes, Sir."

"Then why are you out looking for a job?" Bill inquired. "Rusty has more work at Clark's Woodworking than anyone in town."

"I've been working there," Benji admitted, "but I just wanted to get out and try it on my own. So I quit that job and moved out into my own apartment."

The interviewer suspected what the problem was but didn't mention it to Benji. "Well, I could use someone around here handling materials, cleaning up, and running errands. It pays minimum wage, if you want it," Bill offered..

I guess that will have to do, Benji thought. "Okay, I'll take it." But he thought that it would be only for a short time, for he believed that his parents would give in soon and beg him to come home.

"Let me tell you the conditions of employment here," Bill Johnson said. " No drinking or drugs. That means no coming in here in the morning with a hangover either. You will have to be here promptly at 8:00 and give a full day's work for a full day's pay. Understood?"

"Yes, Sir," Benji agreed. " One other thing; I don't have any transportation right now. Do you have a company truck I could drive to and from work?"

"No," Bill answered emphatically. " But I think there is an old bicycle around back you can use if you want to. Can you be here tomorrow morning?"

"Yes, Sir." With pitiful prospects, Benji left for home, unsure if he could work there more than a few days. It was not nearly as good as he had it at his dad's place where he was paid nearly twice minimum wage and furnished transportation.

When Benji was gone, Bill telephoned Rusty to tell him what had happened. "Thank you for giving him a job," Rusty said. "I'll be honest with you and tell you that he became rebellious, quit school and work. He has begun doing things we don't approve of, so we are trying to let him be independent, as he thinks he wants to be. I hope you will not cut him any slack because of our friendship. Make sure he has to earn his pay."

"Oh, don't worry about that. I had already guessed what the problem was," Johnson confessed. "It's just another teenager climbing fool's hill."

That evening none of Benji's friends came by as he expected them to. He began to realize that they were willing to be his friends only if he had money to feed their habits and wheels for their use. He walked to a convenience store and spent half of his remaining money on beer and cigarettes and walked back to spend the evening alone. Even then, Benji knew that he had made some serious mistakes, but he was too proud to admit it to anyone, certainly not to his parents.

Rusty kept up with Benji through friends and his new employer, but otherwise he made no attempt to see him or allow him to know that he was keeping up with him. The family did not see Benji for six weeks although Rusty heard the news about him regularly. At about the six-weeks mark, Benji had a weekend of drinking and smoking marijuana, and when he arrived at work on Monday morning thirty minutes late with his pupils dilated, Bill called him into the office. "Benji, do you remember the conditions of your employment?" Mr. Johnson asked.

"Yes, Sir. I'm sorry about being late. I overslept. It won't happen again, I promise," Benji replied.

"No, it won't happen again here," Bill said. "Even more important, you are under the influence of drugs right now. We can't have that in the shop; you will get hurt or cause someone else to. You have one day's pay coming, so I'll pay you and you will have to leave."

"Thank you. I'm sorry. I guess I don't deserve to work here anymore," Benji muttered.

"Benji, before you go let me give you a bit of advice," Bill offered.. " I've known your dad for twenty years, and I can tell you there is not a better man in town. I don't know what your problem is with him, but you need to think about what you can do to get back into his good graces. He loves you as much as a father can love his children. You wouldn't know this but when you were born Rusty posted pictures of you all over his office walls. You must be breaking his heart now. But I can promise you that he will be as fair to you as any parent I know if you give him the chance."

Benji walked away crying. As he trudged home to the apartment, he knew he had made a big mistake, several of them, in fact. He would like to go home, but he had been so rebellious and determined to make it on his own that he hated to go admit he was a failure. Besides, he was so dependent on drugs that he was not sure he could stay clean; however, without a job now he didn't see any way he could buy them, and his former friends weren't around to supply them to him, and he absolutely refused to become a dealer.

With almost nothing to eat all week, and no money to buy food, Benji knew where he could get a good meal Sunday. His hunger drove him to get dressed and walk to First Church for the morning service. He could see his family near the front when he slipped in and sat on the back pew. Benji remained out of their sight until his dad, serving as an usher, came by receiving the offering. Then when Rusty had returned with the offering plate and deposited it on the communion table, instead of going back to sit with his family, he went to the back row and sat with Benji. Then when the congregation stood for the next hymn, the family saw where he was and followed him and sat with Benji until the service ended. They could tell that he was uncomfortable during the sermon, but he stayed through the entire service, and when the service was over, Benji joined the family in the car to go home with them for lunch. He was thin and looked almost emaciated. They couldn't help but to feel sorry for him.

At the Jenson home they sat down to a delicious meal of beef roast, stewed potatoes, steamed vegetables, and pecan pie. Benji wolfed down food like he hadn't eaten in a week. Every member of the family struggled to keep from crying. "Benji, do you know that we had a birthday last week?" Lauren asked. "Katherine turned sixteen. You had better watch out while on the road because she'll be driving now."

"Gosh, I forgot all about it. I'm sorry I missed the birthday party. Happy birthday, Katherine." Benji sat and visited for a while, but he fidgeted nervously the whole time. When it was time for him to leave he asked, "Dad, since Katherine is driving now, will you let her drive me home? I'd like to see if she is a good driver."

"Okay, but Katherine you be careful and come straight back home."

"May I come in and see your apartment?" Katherine asked when they stopped in front of it.

"Sure, but you'll have to overlook the mess. I've been so busy that I haven't cleaned it."

Once inside, Katherine saw that he was right; clothes were strewn about; dust was on everything; and empty beer cans filled the garbage container.

"I'm sorry I can't offer you anything to drink," he said. "You know I lost my job, and I don't have money for anything. Katherine, I hate to ask but I wonder if you could lend me a few dollars until I find another job. I'll pay you back then."

"Benji, I want to help you" she replied, " but I can't. You have been so blinded by this new lifestyle that you can't see that you are killing yourself. You know the Bible speaks of enjoying the pleasures of sin for a season, but in the end there is disaster. I love you and I don't like what you are doing to yourself. In addition you are breaking Mom and Dad's hearts. Every time we have prayer, Dad prays for you and we all wind up crying. We all want you to repent of your sins and come back to God and home to your family."

"I know I have some problems," confessed Benji, "but I don't know if I can climb out of this pit I've fallen into."

"Look, Benji, if you need to go to a treatment or rehab center, Dad will pay for it. He will get you whatever help you need, but you have to know that no one else can do it for you. Others can help, but only you can change. I know that you have trusted the Lord as your Savior, and I know that He will help you if you turn to Him and ask for help. From what I hear, you've not only lost your job, but you've also lost your friends. They led you into this mess and now they have abandoned you. That's the way of the devil's crowd. Why don't you decide right now to do something about it? If you don't want to go for some rehab, then go to A.A. I don't think you are an alcoholic, but they help people with any kind of addiction. If you will go, then Mom, Dad, and I will go to Al Anon to learn how we can help you. Will you do it for me?" Katherine pleaded.

"I'll think about," he said.

"Okay. I'm going to be praying that you will do more than think about it." With that, Katherine excused herself and drove home. She had been gone less than an hour, when Benji became violently ill. He had to stay in the bathroom with his head over the toilet, apparently because after being without food for so long, he had overeaten and become sick. By midnight, he had lost all of his lunch and still felt too sick to die. Finally, he called out to God; "God if you will hear me, I ask you to help me. Help me over this sickness and help me to turn my life around," he begged. To his surprise, the words just came tumbling out: "Lord, forgive me for my sin. Restore my fellowship with you. I think you are my only hope. I don't want to die away from you. Help me. I beg you, Lord." As he lay on the floor, suddenly a calmness came over him and he fell asleep. When he awoke the next morning, he could hardly believe what had happened during the night. "Thank you, Lord, for helping me. Now please help me to go face those I've hurt and ask their forgiveness," he prayed.

Just before noon, Rusty looked out and saw what looked like a poor homeless man walking toward the shop. Then he got a better look and exclaimed, "It's Benji!" And he ran outside and across the parking lot to embrace him.

"Dad, I'm so sorry. Please forgive me and let me come home. I'll change," Benji promised. " I'm ready to go back to school and…"

Rusty interrupted him and said, "Welcome back, son. You don't know how I've prayed for you and for this moment. Let's get your mom and go home for lunch." They got into the company truck and headed to the nursing home, where they broke the news to Lauren and she grabbed Benji and cried into his chest. "Thank God. You've made me so happy, Benji."

Over lunch they sat around the table and discussed the future. "Do you think you will need to go some place for rehab, Benji?" Rusty asked.

"No, I think with your help and God's I can lick this and be healed. But I do want to go to A.A. meetings for all the help and support they can offer. I promise you that I will never drink or use drugs again; I'll go back to school in the fall; and I'll abide by your wishes. I know I'm not worthy of your forgiveness, but I'll try to earn it," Benji assured him.

"Benji," Lauren spoke up. "I'm so happy for you. I'll make an appointment for you to see the doctor and the pastor this week. Then next week, you can begin working either at the shop or for me at TLC. The best thing you can do for yourself is stay busy and work so hard that you are ready to sleep at night."

"Thanks, Mom. I think I'd like to do something to help others. So if it is all right with you and Dad, I would like to work at TLC. And when I've proven myself, I'd like to go with Dad to the halfway house meetings on Wednesday nights. I think the abuse of alcohol and drugs has been the biggest factor in most of their lives, and I can relate to that. Maybe I can even say something to help them."

"That's great on both counts," Rusty responded. "We can sure use you in both places. Just think, we will be a team again; you with your Mom at TLC and with me at the halfway houses."

Just as their meeting finished, Katherine came in from school and saw a new Benji sitting with his mom and dad, and she ran to hug him, crying. "Welcome home, Brother."

"This young lady," began Benji, "is responsible for my being here. Thank you, Sister."

Benji stayed home over the weekend. It was easy to tell that he was suffering withdrawal pains; he was jittery, couldn't calm down, and had trouble sleeping. To help him, some member of the family stayed with him at all times and engaged him in some activity even if it was no more than walking. Lauren, true to her word, had made appointments for him to see the family doctor Monday morning at 10:00 and the pastor at 11:00. Both men were understanding and offered encouragement and support. The doctor, an aging man of medicine, who had seen many patients with drug and alcohol problems, gave Benji some good advice and a prescription to keep him relaxed through the worst of the withdrawal. Pastor Williams, having known Benji all of his life and known of his recent struggles, expressed appreciation for him, prayed for him, and gave him some reading material that told the story of others who had walked the same road to recovery. Before Benji left the pastor's office, he asked if he could have a few minutes to speak in the Sunday morning service some time after he had proven himself. "I want to share my testimony and ask the church to forgive me for my indiscretion," he explained.

Pastor Williams gladly granted his request and planned it for two weeks later.

As Lauren and Benji left the church to take Benji home, he said, "Mom, can I just go on with you to the nursing home today? I don't think I need to be alone."

"I don't see why not," she responded. "But if you don't feel ready for this, you can wait a few days."

"Thanks, but I need to keep busy, and I'm ready to get started." At the home, Lauren was amazed to see Benji get acquainted with the residents so easily and offer them any help they needed. The seniors were impressed to see a young man willing to do just about anything for them. The little old ladies enjoyed his attention and called on him to push their wheelchairs and take them to dinner. When their day was done and they started for home, Benji commented. "You know there are some wonderful people living at the home, Mom. Some of them have sharp minds yet, and others are just starved for attention."

"Yes, Benji. That's right, but I'm amazed that you have picked up on that so quickly."

Marie had a celebration dinner prepared for the family, and as usual, they all came for dinner at 6:00. After the meal was finished, Rusty took his Bible and read the thirty second Psalms which begins: *Blessed is he whose transgression is forgiven, whose sin is covered. Blessed is the man unto whom the Lord imputeth not iniquity, and in whose spirit there is no guile (Vs. 1-2 KJV)*. Afterward he led the family in a prayer of thanksgiving, and Benji said, "Thanks, Dad, for choosing that Psalm. It describes me."

"It describes every Christian, son."

"I guess you are going to want your Jeep back now that I've just begun driving it," Katherine quipped.

"No, not yet. I can ride to work with Mom, and to church with the family, and if I need to go anywhere else, you can chauffeur me," Benji responded. "Dad, will you go with me to the A.A. meeting at the church tomorrow night?"

"Sure, Son. I'll call tomorrow and find out the time it meets."

When they arrived Tuesday, Benji was surprised at some of the men who were there, people he would not have suspected of having a problem. After the opening prayer, they began to introduce themselves, "Hello, I'm Bill, and I'm an alcoholic"; "Hello, I'm Albert, and I'm a drug addict," and so it went around the circle. When it came Benji's turn he paused, then admitted, "Hello, I'm Benji, and I have a problem with alcohol and drugs." The meeting was informative and inspiring. The men all encouraged Benji and thanked Rusty for joining them for the meeting.

Two weeks later, Benji's name appeared in the Sunday morning bulletin with "testimony." Although he was nervous, he was determined to speak to the church. "I'm sorry," he began. "I've brought shame on my church, my family, and worst of all, my Lord. Most of you probably know that I was saved at home and made my profession of faith, was baptized, and became a member of First Church several years ago. Since then, I've strayed and got into drug and alcohol use. I could easily blame others, but it was my fault. I wasn't strong enough to resist the temptations, so I made the bad choices. I'm asking for your forgiveness. I've already asked for God's and my family's and I believe I have it. When you have forgiven me, I hope to also be able to forgive myself. To all of the young people here, let me warn you of the dangers of drugs. You may not think beer drinking will harm you, but it is just one step in a downward spiral. Drug and alcohol use will draw you away from God, from your church, from your family, and from your self-esteem. Don't do it! And if you are using already, ask God now to forgive you and to help you overcome the problem. Thank you."

"Thank you, Rusty," the pastor responded. "That's a more powerful sermon than I could ever preach. In fact, I'm not going to preach. Let's have an altar call. Come to the altar and pray, confess any sin in your life, re-commit your life to God, and pray for others who need a miracle from God." As the organist began to play, the altar filled with young people and the adults made room for them to kneel. Many came to the pastor and made commitments to God before him. It was the most moving experience anyone had ever witnessed at First Church.

Two weeks later, Benji asked, "Dad, can I go with you to the halfway house Wednesday night? I just want to observe at first. Do you think the residents will mind?"

"No, I don't think so. You are welcome to go, of course." Together they met with the men's group, and Benji was surprised to see men not much older than he, and he thought, "But for the grace of God, that would be me in a few years." He had thought he would keep quiet, but before the meeting was over, he was telling his story and what helped him to turn his life around.

"Dad," Benji said on the way home," those are some good men. They just got off on the wrong foot. They may not know it yet, but you are doing them a great favor. I am curious to know why you are doing it."

"I think I'm serving the Lord, Son. I'm visiting men and women in prison and sharing with them the greatest hope available to them." Thereafter, Benji went every Wednesday and soon he and Rusty were dividing the groups and having one meeting for the men and another for the women. They alternated meeting with the groups to lead the Bible study and the group counseling that followed.

CHAPTER 10

One evening as Lauren watched the 10:00 O' Clock news, she saw a human interest story in which a New Orleans woman stood at the entrance to a park holding up a placard, such as picketers might hold, which asked, "Can you help me to find my daughter, born March 20, 1998?" followed by a phone number. Without knowing why, Lauren was drawn to the story. She had a strange feeling that this would somehow affect her life. Then the next day she saw a preview announcement on the national news that the woman would be interviewed by Ann Curry that night, and Lauren asked Katherine to watch it with her.

"Mom, I have homework to finish," Katherine complained.

"It won't take long. Come watch it with me," Lauren urged her.

"Okay, but I might be doing homework as we watch."

As the special program began, Ann gave a little background, showing the woman holding the sign and then the sign stuck in the ground and left there after the woman went home. She told how the story had aired on a New Orleans station prompting the national network to follow up on it. The interview began with Ann asking, "Nancy Witherspoon, can you tell us what led to this event?"

"Yes, sixteen years ago, I gave birth to a baby girl on March 20, 1998, and left her in a cardboard box on a bench near here in this park in New Orleans, and I want to locate her."

"What is her name?" Ann probed.

"I don't know. I didn't give her a name."

"Was she born in a hospital?"

"No. I was homeless and sleeping in an abandoned tool shed in the park at the time. I gave birth to her there, without any assistance except for another homeless woman who was kind enough to stay with me and help with the delivery," Nancy said.

"Did you have any prenatal care?"

"No. I was too ashamed to go to a doctor and I had no money to pay one," she confessed.

"Can you tell us how you came to be in this situation?" Ann asked.

"Yes," Nancy responded. "My family lived in one of the New Orleans suburbs. I was in an abusive home environment, so when I was seventeen, I ran away. I had no job or place to live. When I became too hungry I ate at homeless shelters and slept at the Salvation Army. Without friends or family, I was glad to find a group of young people who took me in. They were drug addicts and drug pushers but they had a house and I was given a bed to sleep in. Unfortunately, one of the requirements for staying there was to engage in sex with the men. After a week, I couldn't take it anymore, so I left. Then, like other homeless people, I slept in abandoned buildings, under bridges, or on the streets. I sometimes had to beg for food. Six weeks later I began to feel different and I suspected that I might be pregnant. I didn't know what to do."

"Did you consider abortion? You know there are abortion clinics in New Orleans," Ann suggested.

"Yes, but I had no money to pay for an abortion. Finally, I learned of a place where I could get one for free, and I went there to talk to them. They encouraged me to have it, telling me that well over a million women have abortions every year and that half of them are single as I was. 'There is nothing wrong with it,' they insisted. But, even though my life was not pure, I believed in God and I felt that abortion was wrong; however, I promised that I would think about it. As I left the rundown clinic, two women on the street, who were obviously pro-life, approached me and asked me if I would like to see an ultrasound of my baby. They promised me lunch if I would go with them for the test. Being hungry and curious about my baby, I went, and they took me to a doctor's office where an ultrasound was performed and I was shown the live embryo growing in me. They said it was a girl. I felt then that she was a live person, so I knew it would be wrong to kill her. I couldn't do it, so I decided I would keep her and take care of her somehow," Nancy explained.

"But didn't you fail to provide her the care she needed?" Ann asked.

"Yes. it's true that I didn't see a doctor for prenatal care, but I managed to get enough food for a healthy diet. When people saw my condition, they were more than willing to give me food money. Then I found the abandoned tool shed in the park and stayed there until the baby came. A park ranger discovered that I was staying there, but he made no effort to evict me. People picnicking in the park threw away enough food to feed lots of people, so I just had to rummage through garbage cans to find it."

"Why did you give up you baby," Ann asked compassionately.

"I didn't want to, but I had no way to take care of her," Nancy answered, on the verge of tears. "I knew she would be better off with anyone else than she would be with me. I saw people wearing fancy exercise clothes and expensive running shoes in the park regularly early in the morning, and I knew they were able to take care of her, so I took my baby right after she was born and wrapped her in a warm blanket and put her in a cardboard box and left her on a park bench alongside the jogging trail where someone was sure to see her. Then I hid behind a tree and watched until someone came and took her. He saw me and ran after me, almost catching me, but I managed to escape into the trees."

"That sounds like the story of Moses in the Bible," Ann suggested.

"Yes, that is where I got the idea. I remembered my mother reading me that story many times," Nancy said.

"Have you ever regretted giving up your daughter?" Ann inquired.

"I have regretted having to give her up, but I don't regret that I gave her a better life."

"How do you know that she has had a better life?"

"I think that anything would be better than what I could do for her then," Nancy answered.

"Why are you trying to find her now then?" Ann asked.

"I have thought about her every day since I left her, so I would just like to find her and meet her and explain why I had to give her up. I know she must have a better life than I could have given her, and I wouldn't want to take her away from it. But I have to find her and get to know her before I die," Nancy said, with tears streaming down her cheeks.

Ann concluded the interview thanking Nancy for her story and announcing that her phone number would be on the television screen for anyone who might know this sixteen-year-old girl to call.

"Did you hear that, Katherine?" Lauren asked. "That girl was born in New Orleans and has the same birthday as you. Do you think you could be her daughter?"

"No, I'm your daughter. I have no other mother or father," Katherine responded curtly.

"Katherine, you know we told you years ago that you are our adopted daughter. You were not born to us but we chose you because we wanted you. You will always be our daughter, but I just wondered whether you might want to meet you birth mother," Lauren explained.

"No," Katherine protested. "There must have been many girls born in New Orleans on that same day. I'm not her daughter, and I don't want to even talk about it. If you will excuse me, I'm going to my room to finish my homework," Katherine said. But Lauren had scribbled down the telephone number and noted the similarity of facial features Katherine shared with Nancy Witherspoon. She decided that she would not go against Katherine's wishes, but she would like to investigate the matter if her daughter ever agreed.

A week past and Katherine had not mentioned anything about Nancy Witherspoon, so Lauren decided to bring up the subject again. "Katherine, have you thought any more about contacting the mother in New Orleans?" she asked.

"No! Even if she is my birth mother, I am not interested is meeting her."

"May I ask why not?" Lauren asked.

"Whether she is my mother of not, she threw her baby away like a piece of garbage. That's not much of a mother in my opinion. She doesn't deserve to know her daughter," Katherine insisted angrily Lauren had never seen Katherine so adamant about anything before.

"You know we don't know all of the circumstances, but whatever they were, I'm surely glad she left her baby there and that you became our wonderful daughter."

Lauren had recorded the mother's interview on the DVR, so in a few weeks she asked Katherine to watch it with her again. "Do you think you favor her?" Lauren asked.

"Maybe. Look, Mom, since you are so interested, you may call her if you wish, but I think you will find that she is not my birth mother and even if she is I'm not interested in talking with her or meeting her." With Katherine's reluctant permission, the next day Lauren called the New Orleans number and spoke with a pleasant sounding woman. "Hello, this is Nancy Witherspoon." Lauren's first impression was that this sounded like a woman she could be friends with. Lauren introduced herself and explained that they had seen the interview and wanted to know more of her story.

"Thank you for calling, Lauren, but I'm afraid there isn't much more to tell than what you saw on the program. May I ask why you are interested? Do you know someone who might be my daughter?" Nancy asked, with excitement showing in her voice.

"Well, I have an adopted daughter who was found on a park bench in a cardboard box in a New Orleans park, on March 20, 1998. I have no idea whether she is your daughter or not, and to be frank with you she is really not interested in finding or knowing her birth mother. And I don't know that we could ever determine if you two have a connection short of doing DNA tests, but I don't think she would ever agree to that," Lauren explained.

"I can give you one clue, I think," Nancy offered. "My baby had a birthmark about the size of a quarter on her right shoulder blade. I don't know whether it would still be there or not, but it was there when she was born. Lauren was shocked, for Katherine had such a birthmark. She was so self conscious about it that she refused to wear a swimsuit or a blouse that allowed it to show. "May I have your name, phone number, and address?" Nancy asked.

Lauren refused because she couldn't give it without Katherine's permission and Lauren doubted that she would ever agree. "I'm sorry, but I can't do that; however, if you will give me your address, I'll see if I can send a picture of her to you."

"I understand completely," Nancy responded. "I am happy to give you my address and I would love to see her picture. Even if that's all I ever get,

I'll have something of her." With that she gave Lauren the address in a New Orleans suburb, and Lauren promised to be in touch.

"I enjoyed talking with you," Lauren said, "and I hope you find your daughter."

"Thank you for calling, Lauren. This is the first response I've received."

When Lauren told Katherine about the call, she was very complimentary about the pleasing conversation she had with Nancy and asked if she could send a picture. "I don't want you to," Katherine answered. But when Lauren told her about the baby's birthmark, she seemed a bit more interested, for it described her own. Finally Katherine agreed that her mother could send the picture and retrieved a school picture from her bedroom and handed it to Lauren who placed it an envelope with a note of appreciation for their phone conversation and wishing Nancy success in finding her daughter and put it in the mail the next day.

CHAPTER 11

Nancy Witherspoon watched the mail every day for some correspondence from Lauren. So when a letter without a return address finally came, she nervously tore it open and the picture fell out. When she looked at it she broke into tears and kissed the picture. Katherine was a mirror image of her twin sister, Heidi. Nancy read the note, then held the picture and looked at it until Heidi came home from school. Heidi saw that her eyes were red as if she had been crying and asked, "What's wrong, Mom?"

"Nothing is wrong, Heidi. I'm just so happy. Look what came in the mail today." When Heidi saw the picture, at first she thought it was a picture of herself. The girl in the picture had the same dark hair, smooth skin, and upturned nose. "She is your twin, Heidi. She has to be," Nancy argued.

"Mom, you've never told me that I have a twin or anymore about your story. All I know about it is what I saw on television and you didn't mention a twin. For as long as I can remember, we've always lived in a nice house and had enough for a comfortable life, so I had no idea about your homelessness. I never knew I had a twin. You didn't even tell that to Ann Curry," Heidi responded.

"I know, Honey," Nancy admitted. "I was just trying to protect you from the publicity. But I'll tell you the whole story now if you wish. When I was pregnant, I was determined to keep my baby; then when I had twins, I knew there was no way that I could keep two of you. So it was then that I decided to give one to someone else and make them happy and they could give her a better future. For some reason I decided to give up the one with the birthmark on her back and keep the perfect one. I don't know what she is like, but I know that she can't be any better than you." Nancy then told her how she had been raised with an abusive, alcoholic father. When he was sober, which wasn't often, he was kind enough and somewhat loveable, but when he was drinking, he beat his wife and slapped Nancy around. He couldn't hold a job for long, so Nancy's mother had cleaned houses to earn enough to provide them food and a rundown place to live. Then, when Nancy turned sixteen, he threatened to put her out on the streets to earn some money as a prostitute, so to avoid that, her mother suggested that she leave. "As much as she loved me, she felt that I would have a better future on my own than under his control," Nancy said. I packed a small bag with a few essentials and walked away one night while my father was at a bar and before he could come home drunk. Mother cried to see me go, and gave me all the money she had and wished me well. 'I'll be praying for you,' she promised, as I walked out of the door."

"How did you survive?" Heidi asked.

Life on the streets was worse than Nancy had told in the interview and she really didn't want to give Heidi the details, but she gave her some of the story. She explained that she was so alone and so afraid that she didn't sleep for days, for fear of those vagrants around her. When she couldn't stay awake anymore, she found a place to sleep on a park bench. Even there some policeman would come along and wake her and order her to move on. If she stayed in sight on the streets at night, she was often mistaken for a prostitute and propositioned or questioned by the police. When a man approached her she soon learned to run away. She found out from other homeless people that she could search the dumpsters behind restaurants and find left over food. "There were some things I had to have money for, especially after you were born, such as diapers, vitamins, food, and clothes for you. For those I begged for money. I hated to use you, but I found that people were much more willing to give if I was holding a little baby. Please know that I was never just trying to just raise money. When I got enough to buy what we needed, I stopped asking," Nancy explained.

"After a few weeks I realized that I had to do something better for you than sleep in the park with you and beg for food. So I started going to Day Care centers to see if I could find a place that would keep you during the day. But when they learned that I had no home address, no job, and no way to pay, they refused to take you. At one place, the lady excused herself and went to make a phone call and I heard her talking to someone telling them she had a neglected baby to report. I took you and ran. Finally I went to a church which operated a day care center and they offered to take you in exchange for my working there part time. I agreed because I could have food for you and be near you. After a few days, they saw that I was a good worker and called me into the office and said, 'We have some clients who work odd hours and need us to care for their babies part of the night. If you are interested in the job, we will feed and clothe your baby and allow you to eat here and sleep in a small apartment in the back. Would you be interested?' I was very interested; I could see you during the day and sleep with you at night. I did that for two years.

"Then there was a gentleman who always came to pick up his infant granddaughter every day. After a while he began stopping to talk with me and finally invited me to go to dinner on my day off. I accepted on the condition that I could take you along. He agreed, and every week after that we had a date. He loved you and me, and six months later he proposed marriage. I would not accept until I told him my sordid story, and fortunately he said, 'I love you regardless of your past and want to marry you.' Even though he was twenty years older than I was, we married and you and I moved into this nice house and he adopted you. He even has a daughter as old as I am, and we became like sisters. He had a good job and earned a good income. He was so good to us, and because of him we have enjoyed a comfortable home and a good family relationship. Unfortunately, as you know, he suffered a fatal heart attack two years ago. However, we can thank him for leaving us this home and his total assets."

"Thank you, Mom, for taking such good care of me," Heidi said with a hug. "I love you even more because of the sacrifices you have made to be a good mother."

With Katherine's permission, Lauren began calling Nancy regularly and she finally gave her the telephone number and address of the nursing home. Although Nancy had not told her of the twin, she sent her a letter and enclosed a picture of Heidi, explaining who she was. Lauren could hardly believe the similarity of the two girls. And when she showed the picture to Katherine, she exclaimed, "She looks just like me!"

"Yes, she is your identical twin. Her name is Heidi Witherspoon. I didn't know about her until today," Lauren said excitedly.

"You mean I have a twin sister?" Although Katherine had not been interested in meeting her mother, she was obviously interested in her twin. "I can't believe I have a sister, a twin sister. Mom, do you think I could go meet her?"

"I'm sure you can, dear," Lauren promised. "I'll give you her phone number and address. You can call and email her and see if we can arrange to go New Orleans for a short visit."

"Okay, I'm going to call her right now," she said eagerly. An hour later Katherine returned to the living room beaming. "She wants to know if we can come to visit and meet her mother. Do you think we can?"

"Yes, we can. When do you want to go?"

'Well, our birthday is coming up, so we thought maybe we could celebrate it together for the first time ever," Katherine answered.

"Look at the calendar and see what day of the week March 20 is on this year."

"I've already looked," she admitted. "It's on Thursday, but if we could be there on Saturday the 22^{nd,} that would be close enough. What do you think?"

"I think that will be wonderful. We will talk to Dad to see if he wants to go and if so, if he can get loose from work."

Rusty felt he was too busy to get away and suggested that they just make it a girls' visit. So Friday, March 21 Lauren and Katherine keyed Nancy's address into the GPS and left right after noon. They made the five-hour trip without incident. As they neared the address, Katherine became so excited that she talked nonstop for the rest of the way. When the GPS had directed them safely to the address, they were amazed at the lovely home. It was a two storey brick home with a beautifully landscaped lawn. Azaleas in full bloom were strategically located around the house and lawn. As soon as they stopped and opened the car doors, a duplicate of Katherine ran from the front door, followed by an attractive, dark haired lady who couldn't have been more than thirty-five years of age herself. She was tanned as if she had been the one tending to the lovely flowers and lawn. Katherine and Heidi ran to each other and embraced as if they had been lifelong friends, but Heidi was more reserved when she shook hands with Nancy. Lauren and Nancy greeted each other warmly and Nancy invited them into the house.

Inside Nancy had a beautifully decorated chocolate cake on the table and a full pot of coffee ready to serve. "Chocolate is Heidi's favorite dessert. I hope you will like it too, Katherine." Both the mothers laughed when Lauren confessed that it was Katherine's favorite too. They sat at the dining table and enjoyed cake and Cajun coffee, a little strong, but with good favor. When they were finished, Nancy suggested, "Let's get your luggage and I'll show you to your rooms where you can rest or freshen up if you like."

"Oh, we don't want to put you to any trouble; we can just stay in a motel," Lauren offered.

"Heaven forbid!" Nancy exclaimed. "You'll stay right here. We're all family." So they brought in their luggage and Nancy showed them to separate bedrooms with adjoining baths. Lauren tried to relax on the bed, but, like Katherine, she was too excited to rest. At 7:00 p.m. Nancy brought out large bowls of shrimp salad. "If you need something else, just let me know. We've stocked up on everything we might need." Lauren was impressed that Nancy prayed before the meal, offering thanks for their safe trip and the food. She tried to serve them more cake but the salad was so large and filling they had to politely refuse.

"May we go to my room now, Mom?" Heidi asked. With permission granted, they ran up the stairs like two children, leaving Lauren and Nancy alone to get better acquainted.

"We didn't know Katherine had a twin sister," Lauren said. "You didn't mention her during the interview on television."

"No, I didn't want to bring unwanted publicity to her. I didn't know how her classmates would react, even though those who know us well will figure it out."

It had been a long day for Lauren, so she excused herself to go to bed at 10:00. As she passed Heidi's room she could hear lots of giggling and popular music playing. Awaking early on Saturday morning Lauren peeked into Katherine's room and discovered that the bed had not been slept in; panicking, she quietly opened the door to Heidi's room and peeped in to see the girls sound asleep, sharing a single bed.

After breakfast, Nancy announced that she had made an appointment for both girls to go to the beauty salon at 10 O'clock for hairdos, manicures, and pedicures, and that Heidi had money for them to go shopping for their birthdays. Being familiar with the town, Heidi drove, zipping them around in her Volkswagen Beetle. By 11:00 they had the same length hair and the same hair style and the same color nail polish. "Where would you like to shop?" Heidi asked.

"Let's go somewhere and buy matching outfits," Katherine suggested. So at a large department store, they found that their interests and sizes were similar and wound up with matching fancy jeans and lovely blouses. When they arrived home, both mothers were surprised, and Lauren teased, "Let me see which of you has the birthmark." By the time came for the Jensons to go home, Heidi and Katherine had made plans for Heidi to come to their home in Winslow for a couple of weeks when school was out for summer. Before they left Katherine hugged Nancy and said "Thank you for doing what you thought was best for me. When Heidi comes why don't you come too?"

"I just might do that," Nancy answered. "I will at least drive her up there since she doesn't feel comfortable traveling that far alone."

"You will be most welcome," Lauren added. Despite a good get-acquainted visit, Nancy still didn't tell Lauren her sad news. That would have to wait for another time.

Heidi and Katherine talked on the telephone and sent text messages every day, still it seemed to them like ages before the summer break came. However, as soon as school was out Nancy and Heidi kept their promise and drove to Winslow. Nancy planned to visit for two days and then leave Heidi there for two weeks. The girls had already planned more than enough activities to keep them busy for the entire time. During her last day there, Nancy told Lauren that she had something important to tell her confidentially.

CHAPTER 12

"Lauren, I have a terminal illness, and the doctor says that I will not live long," Nancy began.

Shocked, Lauren exclaimed, "Oh, I'm so sorry! What kind of illness is it?"

"It's an inoperable brain tumor. I've kept it from Heidi because I didn't want her to worry through her last year of high school. Lauren, I hope this is not asking too much of you, but I wonder if you will be willing to see after her when I'm gone. I know she is practically grown, and she will be financially independent, but she will need someone on whom she can depend; Katherine is the only blood relative she will have left."

"No, it isn't asking too much. In fact, Heidi and Katherine are so much alike that she is almost like my other daughter already. Of course we will take care of her if and when the time comes that she needs us; however, it will be much easier for all of us if she decides to come live with us. Do you think she might?" Lauren asked.

"I don't know," Nancy answered, "but she is becoming so close to Katherine that I think she might want to. I sure hope so. I'm so thankful. She has been my greatest concern. I'm not worried about dying, but I want her to be cared for when I'm gone."

Katherine was spending much of her free time at the nursing home helping out in any way she could. She read to the patients, played board games with them, and played the piano for them. Heidi was excited to accompany her, and together they sang old fashioned favorites and gospel hymns every afternoon. Heidi enjoyed getting to know Benji and often invited him to join them in their activities. Even though she looked like

Katherine, she and Benji were not brother and sister and they didn't act like it either. In fact, Katherine feared that something more was developing between them and she felt a bit jealous.

While in Winslow, Katherine and Heidi visited the local university, and Heidi was so impressed that she decided she wanted to come there to college to be near Katherine. She said that she could live in the dorm and still get to be with her sister often, but Katherine would not hear of her living in the dorm. "You'll live with us," she insisted.

So both of the girls completed the paperwork to enroll in the university after their last year in high school.

Benji was also studying for graduation the next year. He had investigated and found that he could take some needed courses by correspondence from LSU in the summer and they would count for both high school and college credit. Successful completion of those would allow him to graduate high school with the twins in one more year.

After her visit Nancy left to drive home, leaving Lauren to worry that something might happen to her before she made it home. Katherine told her mother that she and Heidi had both decided to attend the local university and that she had asked Heidi to live with them. "Is that okay?" she asked.

"Of course it is. We would much rather have you both here than away in some dorm room at a school far away."

Katherine and Heidi's visit went well; it seemed like the two weeks flew by, but just as it was time for Nancy to return for her, a nurse called from a New Orleans hospital and told her that her mother was hospitalized and that she had asked her to call. "My mother is in the hospital? What's wrong with her?"

"You will have to wait for the doctor to explain it to you. You just need to come home," she added.

"Okay, I'll leave early in the morning. I should be there by noon." Heidi thought she would just hop on a plane for New Orleans until she found out that she would not arrive in New Orleans unto 4 p.m. She knew that someone could drive her there quicker.

"You can't do that anyway," argued Katherine. "I'm going with you. After all, she's my mother too. Together we will be safe. Lauren agreed and suggested, "You can take my car, and when it is time for you to come home I can fly down there and we can drive back together."

When the twins arrived at the hospital, they found Nancy in a coma and in ICU. "What's wrong with her?" Heidi asked every nurse she saw.

"The doctor will be around in the morning and he will talk to you then," they promised.

Katherine reported the situation to Lauren; then the twins stayed in the ICU waiting room all night because they didn't want to miss the doctor the next morning. When the doctored arrived the next morning and started to introduce himself, Heidi rushed to him and demanded to know what was wrong with her mother. "Let's go into this conference room and talk," he suggested. "Has you mother not told you about her illness?" he asked.

"No. What illness?"

"I'm sorry to have to tell you, but your mother has a brain tumor."

"Can't you operate and remove it?" Heidi asked.

"Again, I'm sorry to tell you that it is inoperable. There is nothing we can do about it."

"Is she going to die?" Heidi asked in tears.

"We can't say how long she will live, but, yes, she will eventually die from it; however, we expect her to come out of this coma soon," he explained. Heidi burst into tears, crying uncontrollably. "I will leave you alone for now," the doctor said, "but we will talk again later." Katherine held Heidi in her arms until she had cried out, then called Lauren to break the news to her.

"I'll fly down tomorrow to be with you and Heidi until she is better," Lauren promised. The next morning, she had things to do at the nursing home and made it to the airport just before her noon flight was to depart. By the time she arrived at the hospital later in the afternoon Nancy was conscious and talking. She thanked Lauren and Katherine for coming and said they shouldn't have gone to that much trouble. She said she thought she would be getting out of ICU the next day. However, when a nurse came in to have her stand on her feet beside the bed, her legs collapsed as soon as they hit the floor. If the nurse had not caught her, she would have been in a heap on the floor. It was obvious to all of them that she couldn't stand and wouldn't be getting out the next day.

When the doctor asked to see the family again, he said, "We have done more testing and found that the part of the brain that controls motor skills is affected by the growth of the tumor."

"What does that mean, doctor?" Heidi asked.

"I'm sorry, but it means that she will never walk again, and she will have to have full time care for the rest of her life."

"Do you mean twenty-four hour nurses?"

"Yes, or a nursing home."

"A nursing home. My mother is only thirty-four years old. I thought nursing homes were for old people," Heidi complained. "Can't I just quit school and stay home and take care of her?"

"You don't understand. It will be much more difficult than you think and you can't do it alone," the doctor informed her.

Lauren interrupted, "Heidi, you know that your mother will not allow you to do that. There has to be another way."

"If a nursing home is the only thing left to do, do you know of a good one you can recommend?" Heidi asked him.

"There are a number of them in the city, but, unfortunately, none of them is as good as we want them to be. I can't recommend one over the others. You'll just have to visit them and choose the one you like best," the doctor responded.

"How soon will she be able to leave the hospital?" Heidi asked.

"We will move her out of ICU into a private room tomorrow. You know the insurance companies do not allow us to keep patients long enough these days, so you will probably need to move her out of the hospital within a week." Heidi asked to see Nancy again before she left, and she tried to be positive, telling her that she would get out of the hospital within a week.

"Good," Nancy mouthed. "I'm ready to go home." Heidi couldn't bear to tell her yet that she would not be going to her home.

None of the ladies had eaten all day, and it was dinner time by then. So instead of going home to cook, they went to a family diner and ordered a home-cooked meal. "I have an idea," said Katherine. "If our mother is going to spend the rest of her life in a nursing home, can we take her home to TLC? And Heidi can live with us. What do you think, Heidi? Mom?"

"It's going to be Heidi and Nancy's decision," Lauren responded, "but I think it's a wonderful idea."

"So do I," Heidi said excitedly. "She has no family here and no one that she is particularly close to and no other reason to stay here. Besides, TLC in the best nursing home I know of."

Lauren reminded them that the doctor was going to give Nancy the grim news that evening and that they could give her overnight to think about it and then talk with her about it the next morning. All agreed, so they went home for a good night's sleep. That night in the privacy of her room, Lauren called Rusty and told him about the situation. No sooner had she said nursing home than Rusty interrupted with, "TLC. Bring her up here where we can help take care of her and Heidi." Lauren knew he would be agreeable but to hear him suggest it before she even mentioned it was confirmation that this must be the right thing to do.

The next morning they found Nancy in a private room with a worried look on her face. "Did the doctor tell you?" Nancy asked. They all nodded. "I'm not worried about myself. This is just the natural progression of the illness. But I am worried about you, Heidi. You don't need to be living alone, and you don't need to be burdened with my care either."

Heidi told her of Katherine's suggestion and their discussion at dinner and asked if she would go to TLC for her care, assuring her that she would receive the best care there. Nancy burst into tears; "You all are just too good to me. I don't deserve it."

"You're my birth mother and Heidi is my sister. And we are committed to helping others, especially our family," Katherine spoke up.

"I would really like that," Nancy said. "We'll have to close up the house until we decide what to do with it. It may be, Heidi, that you will want to come back here to live when you finish college."

"No, Mom. There is too much crime here and always the threat of a hurricane. I decided a long time ago that I would leave New Orleans when I could, so let's just sell it. You are the only thing that could keep me here."

Three days later, when the ambulance pulled into TLC, Rusty, Lauren, Marie, and the twins were there to greet Nancy. Lauren had arranged for Nancy to have a room that had just been vacated, the best private room in the home. Heidi had brought what clothes and personal items she thought her mother would need, so the room was soon made to look like her home. Marie announced that since she didn't have as much to keep her busy now, she was going to spend a good part of each day with Nancy helping to care for her. With most of the family working there, Nancy would not lack for family attention.

After working for an agency for several years, Cathy had decided to go into business for herself. She gave physical therapy in private homes and nursing homes, and because of her dedication and success, she had more requests for treatment than she could take already. However, she agreed to squeeze in one more patient – Nancy. Three times a week she came to work with Nancy and soon had her standing on her own. Nancy's doctor was amazed that she could make any progress, but he had taken a special interest in her care and together they had agreed for her to receive an experimental treatment that was still being tested. That plus Cathy's determination and Nancy's work ethic produced some positive results immediately. Soon she was walking between parallel bars, then with a walker. Nancy knew that it was an answer to prayer, to Cathy's expertise, and to Nancy's hard work.

CHAPTER 13

The halfway houses funded by the Eva Howie Foundation had built such a reputation for success that they were cited as a models for others around the state. Fewer of the residents there caused trouble or had gone back into crime after their release than anyone could believe. Because Rusty and Benji were open with the residents about their own past, they soon had others admitting their guilt and accepting responsibility for their crimes. Both of them were such fervent soul winners, that they soon had a house full of converts. It was interesting to see Rusty walk into church and sit with two pews full of halfway house residents who had come in the van. Because of their good experience with Rusty and appreciation for his help he had to turn away many who wanted to work for him. But he always tried to help them find jobs. In fact, so many other business owners began to call Rusty to find good employees that he began to feel like an employment agency.

Enough of the residents had received Christ as Savior that as soon as a new person arrived they began to witness to him immediately. And some of them were becoming proficient in Bible knowledge and engaged in Bible study groups on their own. Since Rusty's time was limited, he had to make time to manage the foundation, oversee the operation, help locate jobs, and lead his study/counseling sessions on Wednesday evenings. But he considered it a ministry which took precedence over his business, so at work he relinquished more and more of his responsibilities to others.

Of course, not everyone was so open and agreeable. When Isaac, a burly African American, came from a local corrections facility, he announced, "I've heard about your churchy program, but I don't want no part of it.

You do-gooders can take your preaching somewhere else. I may have to sit through some of it, but I'll not participate. Rusty listened to his objections and knew that only God could change his heart and behavior.

"Okay, Isaac," he said. "We are happy to have you here. We don't push our religion on anyone, but you will be invited to attend the religious services and required to take part in the Wednesday night group sessions."

One of the requirements of the program was that each resident work at some job during the day, so Rusty did his best to help them find work. However, Isaac's sullen attitude kept him from being accepted and he still had no work after the first month, so Rusty said, "Isaac, why don't you come to work for me?"

"You mean you will give me a job?" he asked.

"Yes," Rusty said, " have the van to drop you off at Clark's Woodworking tomorrow morning at 8:00."

"I don't know nuthin' 'bout no woodworking," Isaac complained.

"Okay," Rusty said, "you come anyway; we will find something for you to do."

By noon the next day, Isaac had mowed the yard at the shop and swept out the buildings. But as the crew sat at lunch together and carried on the good-natured banter, Isaac sat alone and remained silent. "Come over here, Isaac," Rusty said, and motioned to an empty seat. Reluctantly he moved, but still he said nothing or joined in any of the activities. However, everyone seemed willing to accept him and tried very hard to make him feel welcome. After lunch Rusty assigned him to move and restack some stored lumber supplies, a job which everyone despised but Isaac seemed eager to do it.

The next morning, Isaac approached Rusty and said, "Mr. Jenson, I haven't been completely honest with you. I have done some construction work in the past and I do know a little about the kinds of work you do here."

"Okay," Rusty responded. "First, you can call me Rusty, like everybody else does. Let's see if we can find you a job you feel comfortable with. We usually start new people off with the sanding jobs; I'll get someone to show you what has to be done. How's that?"

"Good. I'd shore like to give it a try." Isaac sanded cabinet door all morning long. By noon he had so much sawdust on him one could hardly tell what color he was. Rusty had no plans, however, to limit him to that job, so he asked the men to each show him the job he was doing and a little about the saws and machines. He seemed to be a quick learner, so by the end of the day he was operating one of the table saws, and his attitude had improved dramatically.

The third day one of the men was climbing around in some of the stacks of lumber looking for just the right kind of material he needed when the lumber shifted and trapped his leg between the heavy stacks. Other workmen saw his plight and ran to try to help him but try as they may they were unable to free him. However, when Isaac saw what was happening, he came running, and with his massive strength, lifted the pile of lumber off of him allowing others to pull him out. Rusty rushed him to the hospital to be checked out, but before they left, the injured man said, "Thanks, Isaac. You're a good man to have around." As it turned out the injuries were not serious, and he was able to come back to work the next day.

Not only did Isaac love working in the shop, he soon became friends with Rusty and the other men. His attitude improved daily both at work and in the home. He confessed to Rusty, "I never thought you would even care about me and then you gave me a job. I know now that I have been wrong, so I'm going to start coming to the Bible study. I grew up under the teachings of a godly grandmother, but crime and jail do something to a man that makes him hard." Isaac became a model resident in the home and he even began going to church on Sundays. He became a mentor to other new residents. Some came in with a big chip on their shoulders and Isaac jumped right in to make friends and lead them to change.

The door and window shop had broadened the scope of its customer base tremendously. An attractive and informative web page gave the businesses more publicity than ever before. And because of the demand in a larger area, Rusty added a delivery truck to cover the northern half of the state. He sent doors, windows and molding to supply houses, and when builders saw the quality of his work, they began to order cabinets from him as well. Additions were made to both buildings and additional workers were added to the overworked crew. However, with more success in the business, the demands on Rusty's time increased also, and it was beginning to show on his health. He didn't complain, but he experienced fatigue all of the time. He knew that he needed to find a way to slow down and rest more.

CHAPTER 14

The following fall, Benji, Katherine, and Heidi were all in the twelfth grade at the local high school. Other students questioned how Katherine and Heidi could be identical twins and yet have different last names. The girls told them no more than that Katherine had been adopted as an infant. The trio was disturbed that recent surveys showed a decline in the number of people in the United States who believed in God, or in Heaven, or that the Devil and Hell are real. Statistics showed that the percentage of believers had dropped considerably during the past eight years, and they feared the numbers were even worse among students. Many of them were searching for meaning in their lives, but, unfortunately, most were looking in the wrong places, for Benji had been among them and seen how they lived. Under Benji's leadership he and the twins decided to try to begin a prayer group before class one morning a week, but when they approached the principal with their idea, he was uncertain about his authority to permit it. However, he took their request to the superintendent of the district, who also seemed afraid to approve it. They then found themselves at the next district school board meeting where they were on the agenda to make their request. And, after some discussion of the legality of it, the board decided to permit it for the last thirty minutes before classes began in the morning. "If anyone challenges your right to do it, we'll let the courts settle it," they promised. The next week they posted notices throughout the building of the meeting on Wednesday morning only to find them torn down by the next day. Nevertheless, when Wednesday morning came they met with about a dozen students. True to their plans, they sang a lively Christian hymn, read a scripture passage, then Benji gave his testimony and they prayed, finishing before the first bell.

Their number doubled for the next meeting. Each week a different student selected a Bible passage and another gave a testimony and a different one prayed. Benji did not want it to be his program, but the students'. Every week their numbers grew and they came to see unsaved and unchurched students attending as well as others, interested in hearing what they had to say. As a result they saw a number of young people saved and the atmosphere at school improve. Unfortunately, many of the girls were more interested in talking with the handsome Benji than hearing his message, and the guys were more interested in the pretty twins.

As usual when something good happens, Satan is always at work to try to thwart God's work. He has been at it since Adam and Eve were in the Garden of Eden. So another group of students requested a space next door to the prayer meeting on the same Wednesday mornings to have a meeting of their own. The principal could hardly refuse since one group had permission. However, it seemed the second group's agenda was only to disrupt the Christian meeting. They played loud music making it difficult for the Christian group to hear their program. Their numbers never grew to be large, but they were effectively interfering with the prayer group. Then a small group, calling themselves the "Atheist club" demanded equal time. Soon the controversial situation prompted the officials to cancel all of the meetings. Not to be defeated, Benji called on the pastor of the church across the street and explained their dilemma and asked if they could meet at the church, and he was happy to provide them meeting space each Wednesday. The only disadvantage was that the students could not leave the school property after they reached it in the morning, so they had to go to the church first then to school.

The next May Heidi, Katherine, and Benji graduated together; the whole family went to the ceremonies. Even Nancy was able to go; Rusty pushed her in a wheel chair to the entrance to the auditorium, but she wanted to walk in and to their seats with the aid of only a walker. All three of the graduates were recognized for their scholastic standings in the class. Rusty had been asked to speak at graduation, probably because he had three family members in the class, so he asked his family if he could use their stories in his address and, since most everyone knew about them anyway, they all agreed. When he walked to the podium, Lauren thought he was so handsome in his dark suit, white shirt, and tie. He began by congratulating the graduates and commending the parents who had provided the support and encouragement for their children to make the achievement possible. "Graduates, we are proud of all of you. Our family is happy to have three graduating with honors tonight. They have faced some challenges as you all have, but you have all reached this important milestone in your lives, and I pray that you will make it a stepping stone to even greater things. I hope you will forgive me for being personal about our family, but I think there may be something to learn from our experiences.

"Katherine and Heidi have told me that some of you have questioned how the identical twins could have different last names. Heidi's mother, Nancy Witherspoon, is with us tonight despite having a terminal illness. She is to be commended, for under unfortunate circumstances, she became pregnant at an early age, but she refused to have an abortion, choosing instead to keep her baby even though she was homeless. However, when she gave birth to twins, she knew that, given her circumstances, she couldn't possibly manage with two babies, so she made a courageous decision like Moses' mother and placed her precious baby on a park bench and secretly watched until someone came along and took the child. To make a long story short, we became the proud parents of that baby and named her Katherine. As soon as she was old enough to understand, we told her that we had chosen her and adopted her, making her our child. Even though she accepted that very well, she must have had the normal questions about who her birth mother was and why she gave her up. Unfortunately, Katherine never knew her birth mother until a few months ago, and the girls never knew about each other or saw each other until then either. But now they are like well, twins.

"I know that I'm not telling you any secrets when I tell you that our son Benji went through a difficult time when he began drinking and using drugs. I can't condemn him, because I had similar problems when I was young. Benji dropped out of school, putting him a year behind his classmates, prompting us to take drastic action. With broken hearts, we put him out of our home rather than enable him to live as he was. But we are so proud of him now, because he, with God's help, has turned his life around, got back in school, and is graduating tonight, with plans to continue his education.

"I'm not telling you this because I think our family is unique or better than any other or that we are the only ones who have faced difficulties in life. I'm telling you because there are some important lessons to be learned from our experiences and to challenge you to safeguard your lives against disaster. Young people, don't engage in the kind of activity that will lead to parenthood until you find that special person for you, fall in love, and marry. There are many temptations; unfortunately some of your peers have yielded to them and will not be happy until they convince you to join them. But I can tell you from personal experience that alcohol and drug use will rob you of your innocence and enslave you. Unchecked, it will destroy you. Because of it I spent five years of my young life in Angola State Prison. I'm not proud of it, and it was only because Jesus Christ saved me by His grace and turned me around that I am here tonight. I challenge you to become all you can be. Set your goals high and strive with all your might to reach them. There are good things waiting to be done in the world and you can be the ones to do them. Don't let yourself, your parents, or your teachers down. Make them proud!" With that Rusty walked off the stage and as he returned to sit with Lauren, the audience rose to their feet applauding. After the graduation, the family enjoyed dinner together at a restaurant, and the young people set out to join some other Christian youth for a graduation party, promising to be home by midnight.

The next evening, after dinner, Bible reading, and prayer, Rusty told all three of the teens how proud he was of them. "Benji," he began, "for more than a year now you've proven yourself. Not once have you asked to have a vehicle, but all of you are going to scatter now, so I think that it's time for each of you to have transportation. Heidi has a good car which she enjoys, and I'm sure Benji would love to drive the Jeep again, so that leaves Katherine needing a car. So, girl, tomorrow you think about it, and you and Heidi can visit some dealerships, and the next day I'll take you to buy a car."

"Do you mean it, Dad? Thank you. I'll be so excited to get out of that Jeep and to have my own wheels."

"Remember," Benji chided, "you have to be responsible or Dad will take it away from you. I'll be glad to get the Jeep back, too."

Two days later, Rusty and the twins went car shopping. He had learned his lesson when he bought their first car without considering

Lauren's wishes and knew never to do that again. So the choice was largely Katherine's. "What kind of car do you like, Katherine?" he asked.

"Well, Dad, we looked at lots of them. Heidi has a small car and it's so easy to maneuver and park, so I want a small one. Since I'll probably have to buy my own gas soon, I want one that gets good gas mileage. And I want something that is going to be reliable, yet attractive."

"Have you found one that meets your qualifications?"

"I think so, but it's pretty expensive. I want a Mini Cooper, and there is one in just the color I want at the dealership," Katherine suggested.

"Okay, let's look at it," Rusty said. When they arrived at the dealership and Rusty saw the car, he thought it was really small, but when he sat in it he was surprised at its roominess and features. "If this is what you want, this is what you will have," he said to Katherine. In a short time she drove away in it, a proud teenager.

By the time Benji was a university student, he had become so confident and self-assured that he had become someone others admired and looked to for an example. His faith in God had kept pace with his maturation, and eventually he came to his dad to ask how one would know it God was calling him into the ministry. "Son," Rusty said, "I always assumed that you would take over our business one day. But I understand that there are more important things to do, so if God leads you in a different way, you follow Him. As for a call to the ministry, I can't answer that question for certain since I've never experienced it. However, I want you to know that I'm extremely proud of your Christian commitment and that you are willing to do what God calls you to do. I think knowing God is calling you must be like knowing that you are in love. You can't explain how you know it, but it becomes the central focus in your life. You just can't get away from it. You begin to feel that there is nothing else you can do. But, Benji, you just need to remember that God calls all of us to be ministers. You don't have to be the pastor of a church to be a minister. A minister is one who does what God leads him to do. In fact, you are a kind of minister now at the halfway house and at TLC." Then he suggested that Benji pray about it, and go talk with some pastors about the matter.

"Dad, you are the best unofficial Christian minister I know," Benji responded. "You seem to make it a way of life, not a special activity."

"Thank you, Son, I guess that pretty much describes my view of the Christian life."

When Benji went to talk with Pastor Williams at First Church, he too agreed that Benji would be an excellent pastor. However, like Rusty, he emphasized that ministry is following God's leadership and doing what He wills. Jokingly he added, "I've seen some mighty good laymen ruined by going into the professional ministry. Seriously, the only thing I can say to you is to do what God leads you to do." By then Benji had come to feel that maybe God was trying to tell him that He had some other way for him to serve. He was still not convinced of what it was; however, he knew that God was calling him to some kind of special ministry.

Benji sat in one university class after another where the professor spoke disparagingly of Christianity. Not all the teachers were guilty of course for some were dedicated Christians, but even they felt that their hands were tied as far as bearing a Christian witness in the classroom. It seemed as if the opposition was free to promote their views, however. When one of his professors said, "There are no gods or demons; we make our own," Benji felt that God had answered his prayers. He realized that his fellow classmates across the land were going to be shaping the spiritual life and mores of this country in the future. Unless they are grounded in the faith, he thought, they will not have a positive impact on the society of tomorow. They are the key to our needs. The question he asked himself was, "What can I do to help shape this generation to lead our world in a godly way?" He didn't have an answer yet, but he knew that it was to be his mission. He looked around and saw that a number of denominational groups operated campus ministries and thought that perhaps that could be the starting place for him.

When Benji began to attend functions at the campus ministry, he discovered that too much of the programming was just aimed at providing a place for fellowship and fun. He decided that he would work to see a greater emphasis on worship, evangelistic outreach across the campus, and helping students to discover their purpose in life. Benji knew that he couldn't change everything suddenly, but that he could slowly influence the activities of the group. Because of his burden to reach the other ninety percent of the students who were not involved in Christian activities, he was asked to be responsible for campus outreach. After accepting the assignment, he began placing posters around campus to inform others of the campus ministry; then he ran an informative ad in the campus newspaper. He enlisted area churches to provide lunch one day a week and engaged young speakers to bring a message. Benji led in the formation of special sessions to help students develop a Christian worldview and to discover their purpose in life. The most basic meeting was planned for non-Christians to help them understand how to be saved and how to have a full and meaningful life. Other Christian students were trained to share their faith and to lead someone else to Christ. In the months that followed, attendance at the ministry doubled, and most felt that it was because of Benji's efforts.

Benji's gifts and commitment were so obvious that he was asked to be the assistant director of the campus ministry and to live in an apartment in the building. Although a student had never been hired for the position before, it was a unanimous decision of the director and the board members. One condition that Benji and the director agreed on was that no student would be allowed to visit Benji in his apartment. If someone needed to talk, Benji was to meet them in the office. At first, he enjoyed the total cooperation of the director, but soon Benji had become more popular among the students than the older man. When they had questions or needed counseling, they came to Benji first. As he feared, the director felt threatened and began to show resentment and jealousy toward him. When he detected the problem, he went immediately to the director and explained that he was not trying to undermine his leadership, and that he was giving total support to him.

"I'm afraid you are trying to take over my job," the director responded. "I cannot allow that to happen, you know, so I'm going to curtail some of your responsibilities. I'll take over the programming, and we will no longer offer some of the things you've been doing. We are not a church, so let's leave the primary responsibility for their Christian training and growth to the churches."

"Sir," Benji, responded, "I respect you and your position. I assure you that I've never tried to interfere with your role, and I will continue to support you completely. But, quite frankly, we have an opportunity here that the church doesn't have. When most students come to the university, they drop out of their local churches. Now, having said that, you know that we have seen lots of growth because of the outreach programs we instituted, and, therefore, I am not willing to stop them. It's not my desire to go over your head, but before I see those activities stopped, I'll take it to the board of directors and ask for their decision on the matter." Knowing of Benji's popularity among the board members and their support of him, the director began to back down and suggested that Benji not try to do that.

Meanwhile Katherine and Heidi were coming into their own. Both were still in the university in different curriculums: Katherine was following in her mother's footsteps to become a nurse, and her goal was to eventually become the administrator of TLC where she still worked part time. But Heidi chose to study business management. They were still best friends, but they were developing separate identities. They no longer dressed alike or tried to look alike. Heidi had begun to work for Rusty at the woodworking shop after classes because her interest was there. Although it was not the normal role for a woman, it was what she wanted to do. She worked in the office every day after class, often visiting out in the shops to learn how the machines worked and how the finished products were made. Katherine had begun to date fellow students, but Heidi was not interested in any of the students except one and she wasn't sure if he was interested in her. However, every time she saw Benji, her heart raced and some strange feeling arose in her. She didn't know if it would ever be proper for her to have anything but a brother-sister relationship with him, but she couldn't stop that special feeling for him.

Meanwhile, Nancy's health had improved remarkably. The local doctor's experimental treatment was reducing the size of the tumor. She had improved enough that she could walk carefully without the walker. Cathy continued with her therapy, and Nancy had begun to make herself useful with the other patients. In fact, when Marie and Lauren suggested that she might want to come live with them, she declined, saying, "I feel at home here and useful. May I just stay here?" They all suspected that her decision had something to do with the disabled veteran, Ray Freeman, with whom she was spending a lot of time, but she often helped other residents with their games and activities too.

Cathy's family had grown beyond her imagination. She now had three children who kept her busy taking them one place or enough. She thought she could hardly wait until they reached driving age and could take some of that responsibility. Little did she know of the pressure that would put on her. When they began to want a car of their own and to go all of the time, she would have new worries that she hadn't considered yet. She scolded herself for wishing they were older and promised herself that she was going to enjoy their formative years as much as she could. They were all good children, but she knew that one day she would have to loosen the ties a bit.

The entire Jenson family attended First Church and usually sat together. Lauren began to notice that Heidi and Benji always wound up beside each other, and when they sang their voices blended very well. Sunday lunches were special events when Cathy and her family and Lauren and hers came together for the meal and a time of visiting. Some Sundays they brought Nancy from TLC to enjoy lunch with them. Usually the university students had school projects to complete and often worked together to get them done. Benji was always pleased when he and Heidi could work together. While everyone else noticed what was happening between them, Benji seemed oblivious to it. Finally, he too began to realize how much he enjoyed being with Heidi and wondered if she was becoming more than a sister to him. He decided that he would just have to avoid the association with her and prevent the attraction.

CHAPTER 15

While Benji questioned the wisdom of spending time with Heidi, he longed to be with her. One day after classes and work she asked to talk with him privately. So he invited her to stop by the ministry office. She came in as cheerful as she could be, for she always seemed thrilled to talk with Benji. "Hey, Sis, he greeted her."

"I'm not your sister," she responded quickly, "and that is my main problem. I feel like something is happening between us that probably shouldn't. I don't know how you feel, but I have deep feelings for you and I don't know how to turn them off. Even though it's my sister who is your adopted sister, we are not allowed to experience more than a brother-sister relationship. While I'm afraid we shouldn't feel more, I can't just turn it off. What are we going to do?"

"I share those same feelings for you," Benji responded. "I've thought and prayed about it a lot but I don't have an easy answer. Why don't we just keep our distance from one another and see what happens. You should date other guys, but I'm so busy that I don't have time for that. Because I'm convinced that God has called me into the student ministry, I know I'll have to get some seminary training to ever be full time in it; therefore, I've recently enrolled in two seminary classes online."

"I don't know of any guys I'd want to date," Heidi asserted. "But I'll try to keep my distance from you, if you're sure that's what you want. I hope we can still be friends, though."

"Of course, and I'll still see you around campus, at church, and at the family gatherings. But it's not really what I want either." They agreed to pray about the matter, and before they parted Benji prayed for God's guidance for them in dealing with the problem. Heidi managed to hold back her tears until she reached her car, but then the floodgates opened. As much as she cared for Benji, she couldn't believe that he could be so quick to close the door on their relationship and suggest that she date others. However, she felt that was what he had just done. She sat in her car and cried until there were no more tears and then made her way home.

When Heidi said she didn't want dinner and went straight to her room, Katherine knew something was wrong, so after dinner, she knocked on her door and asked if she could come in. Heidi's eyes were still red and she wasn't her usual bubbly self. "What's wrong, Heidi," she asked.

"Why do you think something is wrong?"

"I can tell that you are sad, now what is it?"

"I can't tell you," Heidi mumbled. "It's personal, and I had rather not talk about it."

"Okay, I'll respect your privacy, but when you are ready, I'll be here to listen." Heidi didn't come out of her room all evening. And when Katherine went to bed she prayed for her and that she would open up and share her burden. Still, a week passed before Heidi was bursting to talk to someone, and who better, she thought, than her own twin.

"Katherine, I think I'm in love with Benji," she blurted out one evening as they visited in her bedroom.

"Oh, you can't be! He's like your brother."

"But he isn't my brother. He's your adopted brother," Heidi argued.

"Have you talked with him about this? Does he know how you feel?" Katherine asked.

"Yes. And he has feelings for me too, but he said we have to keep our distance and that I should date other guys."

"How do you feel about that, Heidi?" Katherine inquired.

"I don't like either suggestion," she responded. " I just can't stand it when I don't see him, and there is no one else I would want to date. I almost feel like that I would be unfaithful to Benji if I did."

"Have you talked with anyone else about this?"

"No, and you must promise me that you won't tell anyone either. Not your mom and dad or anyone. Okay?" Katherine pleaded.

"Okay, if that is what you want."

"Tell me what you think about it, Katherine?"

"I haven't given it any thought, but I promise you that I will pray about it. Right now, I think it's wrong for you to even feel that way about Benji. I don't think you could ever marry. It would be almost like incest to me. I think Benji's advice is good. Why don't you accept some of those invitations to date you get all the time?"

Heidi had made friends with many students, both male and female, at the student ministry activities. The young man she was closest to, Dan, had asked her for a date many times, but had given up because she would never accept. Now, under pressure to date someone, she decided to ask him if the invitation was still open, and he was thrilled. They agreed on a movie and set the date to meet at the ministry building Friday night. At 6:00 they met and headed out to the Pizza Barn for dinner then to a movie. Dan was a nice young man, polite and fun to be with, but when he asked if they could go together, she declined, saying she was not ready for a permanent relationship. However, at the worship service Tuesday night, Dan came and sat with her. It was obvious to everyone, including Benji, that he was interested in her.

When Benji saw them together, a wave of jealousy hit him hard: he was angry that he couldn't be with her, that he had advised her to date, and that she could be seen with someone else. However, when other young men learned that she had accepted a date with Dan, they too felt they had a chance with her, so she had numerous requests and accepted some of them, but never for a second date with the same guy. Every time she went out she tried to make sure Benji saw her. Maybe she wanted him to be jealous and realize that he was losing her.

Heidi wanted an ally and thought that maybe her mother would side with her, so she took Nancy out to dinner to discuss the situation and use her as a sounding board. Nancy listened patiently and considered the possibilities before answering. "I'm sorry," she began. "Benji is a fine young man, and I don't think you will find a better one, but I don't think it is wise for you to form a romantic relationship with him because he is like your brother. What would people think? What would his parents think? Do they know about this?" Nancy asked.

"No, and you are not to tell them either. When we want them to know we will tell them. Benji is the kind of man I want to date and eventually marry. I've been out with a dozen boys now, and I've been propositioned, called a prude, barely fought off rape, been abandoned, and had to leave and find another ride home. I couldn't muster any interest in any of them, even those who were gentlemen. I don't think I can ever be satisfied with anyone else. I'll probably just stay single all of my life," Heidi grumbled.

Nancy felt the greatest sympathy for Heidi and told her so. Her advice was to stop this infatuation with Benji before it became any more serious. "Give yourself some time," she urged. "You are young with plenty of time before you need to make lifelong commitments. Maybe you'll change your mind in time." Disappointed that she couldn't get the answer she want from someone, Heidi drove her mother back to TLC and then herself home to cry herself to sleep as she had so many other nights.

Benji struggled with his emotions and decisions as well. Questions troubled his peace of mind. He wondered if he should go against his own concerns and date Heidi. What would others think? he wondered. Should he base his decision on what others think or his feelings? Could he continue in this ministry if others thought what he did was wrong? If he had to make a choice between Heidi or the ministry, which would he choose? He knew that there was a right answer and that it was not to be found in his emotions but in God. He still had no clear answer from Him, but he continued to pray for one.

It was time for another talk with Heidi, so Benji invited her to a picnic in the park on Saturday evening. He picked up burgers, drinks and fried apple pies and joined her at a scarred picnic table in the shade of a large oak tree. The visit was very enjoyable with fun-filled conversation, until Benji brought up the matter of their feelings. When he asked Heidi if she had been thinking and praying about it, tears came to her eyes, and he wanted to take her into his arms and hold her but he knew better. "Yes," she answered, "I've prayed, I've cried, I've dated other guys, I've talked to Katherine and my mother, but gotten no where."

"What did Nancy and Katherine say about it? he inquired.

"Both of them disappointed me. They say we can't do this, that it wouldn't be right, but I don't see why not."

"Public opinion is very important," Benji conceded. " But I think they fail to see it as we do. Not only are we unrelated, but we've known each other for only a few years. For me, however, it might mean the choice between what I believe God has called me to do and what I want to do," Benji confessed.

"My mother advised me to give it some time, that things change with time," Heidi said, "but my love will not change. I don't think I can ever love someone else as I do you. If we can't marry someday, I'll just remain an old maid. And, Benji, I don't believe God's will is based on public opinion, and I don't believe that the choice is between your happiness or the ministry. He just hasn't shown us the way yet. Maybe we need this conflict with this problem in order to grow in Him. This may be unrelated, but my English teacher read us William Faulkner's acceptance speech when he was awarded the Nobel Prize for Literature in 1950. He said something like, 'The problems of the human heart in conflict with itself… alone can make good writing because that is all that's worth writing about.' I don't know about you, but I'm having enough of that inner conflict for the both of us." When the time came to leave, Benji took Heidi's hands in his across the table and they prayed. He thanked God for Heidi and for the love they felt and asked God to guide them in their decisions. Sniffling, Heidi prayed that God would make a way for them to be together.

Benji and Heidi graduated in the spring commencement, he with a secondary education degree and she in business management. Katherine had to stay longer to complete her nursing practicum, but she celebrated with them as if they had all graduated. Their parents were so proud of them and they were proud of each other. When Benji and Heidi met in a congratulatory hug something more passed between them that they didn't want to end.

Sam Cox had announced that he would be retiring from the student ministry at the end of summer, and the Board of Directors asked Benji to become interim director with the promise of the permanent position if he continued his seminary education. Though he hadn't told his family, Benji had already enrolled as a full time student in New Orleans for the summer, so he announced that to everyone as they shared a meal together after graduation. Everyone seemed happy and wished him well, but Heidi dropped her head so they would not see her tears and soon excused herself to head to the ladies room.

Early in June Benji packed his car with the belongings he would need for the summer and told everyone that he would come home sometime during the summer if possible, but that he would be back by the fall semester for certain. When he had time to speak a word with Heidi alone, he said, "Heidi, this will be a good test for us. Let's see how we will feel in September."

"I don't need the test," she insisted, "I know how I feel. May I write to you this summer?"

"Yes, please do. I'll probably be pretty homesick. You know, I've never been away from the family for this long before."

"I'm sure your parents will be down there to see you, and I'll be hitching a ride with them if they will let me."

As planned, Rusty gave Heidi the job of business manager at Clark's Woodworking, and soon she had added a computerized system in the business and made some other profitable suggestions. She showed an interest in everything about the business and all of the employers liked her. Soon she asked Rusty for some time to discuss some issues about the business, and, after a brief visit she jumped right in with her suggestions: "We're often asked if we can install cabinets, but most of the time we simply turn the job over to some contractor after we have manufactured the cabinets, and sometimes he doesn't do it right. Why don't we establish a small contracting business? We could take on the job of remodeling kitchens or houses. We would be able to do work for TLC and the halfway houses as well as accept other jobs. Furthermore, since we are in the business of helping people, what if we found retired plumbers, electricians, and painters who would still like to work part time to supplement their retirement income and hire them to do our work instead of using subcontractors?"

"You've given this a lot of thought, haven't you, Heidi?" Rusty asked.

"Yes, I have, and I think we can make it a profitable business and help others at the same time" Heidi argued.

"Let me think about it for a few days and we will talk more about it," Rusty suggested.

"Oh, there is one more thing," Heidi added. "We need a new office, separate from the noise and dust of the shops, and if we start this new venture, we will need it even more. It could be the first assignment of the new crew."

By the next week, Rusty had decided to accept Heidi's recommendations. "I'm going to turn this project over to you, Heidi," he said. "Choose one of our present employees to manage it and see if we can find others to work for us. I also want your suggestions for a name for the new business."

"I think I have it," she said. "How about Master's Contracting?" It will suggest the quality of work we plan to do and our commitment to Jesus as Master."

"That sounds good to me," Rusty agreed. " I'll see Mr. Albertson about getting the paper work done."

By the first of July, Rusty was suffering with chest pains, and when Lauren finally dragged him to the hospital for tests, he was found with blockages which required by-pass surgery to correct. It was serious enough that the doctors refused to allow him to go home, but scheduled the surgery for the next day. Benji drove home that night and the family gathered around his bed early in the morning and prayed for a successful procedure and speedy recovery. Pastor Williams and some of the church leaders sat with the family during the surgery and thanked God for its success at the end. Heidi was not happy about the surgery except that it gave her a chance to see Benji briefly.

Heidi had to get back to the business because she would be responsible for its complete operation until Rusty was able to return, and Benji had to get back to his demanding studies, but he managed to drop by and visit with Heidi for a few minutes and thank her for the frequent letters she sent.

Lauren took a week off work when Rusty was released from the hospital to be sure that he followed orders to take care of himself and to provide the excellent nursing he would need. But a week later he was moving around freely so she went back to work. Marie was still there and he persuaded her to drive him to the shop for brief visits and to sit at the nursing home for a while. A month later Rusty was back in the office with orders to stay out of that shop, and Heidi made sure that he did.

Through the experience both Rusty and Lauren came to the decision that business was not the most important thing in their lives. They decided to depend more on the professional staffs they had in place and to do some other things that reflected their priorities. Rusty wanted to go assist with the annual revival held at Angola, and he began accepting invitations to share his testimony in churches. Lauren made plans for them to go on some overseas mission trips. They decided to expand the halfway houses by purchasing a large old planation home, remodel it and name it "City of Hope." When the new contracting firm was in place that would be one of the jobs for it.

Meanwhile Katherine was settled in at TLC and dreaming of ways they could better serve the Lord and people. After dinner one evening she opened the discussion about her dreams. "Mom and Dad, I have been reading about elder care, and I want to get your opinion on some things. There are lots of elderly people who are staying with their families who need care while their family members work during the day. What if we opened a day care for seniors that would provide a safe place for them. We would need a separate building, but it could be on the grounds with TLC, and we would need some more staff. However, we could utilize some of the ones we have already, such as janitorial, limited nursing, and transportation to the doctor."

"I think that's a wonderful idea," Lauren said. "Do you think it would pay its own way?"

"Yes, I believe it will. But that's not all. I know we couldn't do this all at once, but in some places there are progressive senior services that eventually lead to nursing home care. Could we think about some retirement cottages for seniors to rent that would allow those who are able to maintain their independence but offer them some support. We would need to acquire some property a little farther from TLC, but not so far that we couldn't check on them. For example, we could call them every day, and if they were sick, we might send a nurse to check on them. We could provide them a meal plan if they chose. The next step would be assisted-living apartments for those who need a little more care. And finally, when their health demanded it, the nursing home. What do you think?"

"I think it would require a large investment," Rusty responded. "But I'm impressed with your dreams of providing for different groups of our seniors. I think we may live to see a day when we would need all of those. How could we finance all of this?"

"Well, I believe there may be some government grants we could get to help. And if we were to do it, your contracting firm would have another job," Heidi suggested.

"Which one would you start with," Lauren asked.

"The day care."

"Okay, you check on funding and costs, and we will all pray about it," Rusty concluded.

CHAPTER 16

When Benji came home before the fall semester began he was already enrolled in some online courses from the seminary, so with all of the startup activities at the university and his studies, he was very busy. The young interim director was popular with the students, especially the young girls; however, he always treated them professionally. Fortunately, he didn't have to live in that in-house apartment anymore, so he opted to rent his own apartment close to the university, and arranged for a mature student to live in the apartment rent-free for watching over activities at the ministry.

Benji planned a daunting list of activities for the semester. In addition to the outreach, worship, and Bible study groups he had organized the year before, he wanted to have a four-day revival, called Renew, Revitalize and Re-commit, each semester with an outstanding speaker and dynamic testimonies and inspiring music. Then he planned to train groups of students to be able to lead others to Christ, music groups who would be able to accept invitations to sing in area churches, mission groups who could minister locally or in distant places in the summer, a staff of VBS workers who would be available to small churches who lacked enough workers to do a school on their own. Benji knew that he couldn't do all of these things by himself, so he began to share his plans with others and select from them some capable Christians to be leaders.

Benji became a popular speaker in area churches sharing with them the story of the student ministry and enlisting their prayer and financial support. That meant that he seldom made it to First Church with his family or to see Heidi. Since she had graduated, she didn't visit the student ministry activities often, but as often as possible he and the twins met for dinner together. He and Heidi talked with the Lord often about their relationship but hardly ever to each other alone. It was obvious, however, that the flame still burned in both of them. Neither of them dated, using their busyness as an excuse.

The program at the student ministry was so successful that by mid-year the board of directors named Benji as the fulltime director with the understanding that he would complete his seminary studies in the next three years. Other than some pesky problems occasionally, the student ministry was doing well. Attendance at the scheduled activities had doubled in the fall semester. Study groups had formed independently, and some strong leaders had emerged from the student body. Dozens had been saved, and the revival was deemed a great success.

When the state director of the student ministry for the denomination scheduled a retreat for all of the directors around the state, Benji was asked to share their success story with his colleagues. After his presentation, he was bombarded with questions, the most frequent of which was, "How do you have time to do all of these things?" His answers were, "I'm not married; I don't date; I don't play golf; Christ is first in my life; the student ministry is a close second; and I sleep less." Before leaving the retreat setting, the state director called Benji aside and told him that he would be retiring in three years and that he would like to groom him for the position.

"These other directors need someone like you who can direct and inspire them to do their best where they serve," he argued.

"Thank you for the compliment," Benji replied, "but my first answer is 'no.' I may change my mind later but my interest is in working with the students not their directors. When I grow older and have less energy my answer may change, but not now. Besides, Winslow is home; my family is here, and I wouldn't want to leave."

"We can probably arrange for you to work from here. You would be communicating with directors all over the state and doing some traveling, but you could live anywhere. And your salary will be a lot bigger than it is now."

"I'm sorry," Benji said, "but my answer is still 'no'."

Benji decided that he had to talk with someone about his feelings for Heidi, and he had more confidence in his dad than anyone else, so when

Rusty came in from his latest trip, Benji went to see him and talk with him privately. In his dad's home office he unloaded his burden. "Is it wrong for me to love my adopted sister's sibling? Would it be wrong for us to marry?" he wanted to know.

After listening silently to Benji's questions, Rusty replied, "Others will think that it is wrong and you'll find yourself having to defend your actions. There is no way you can hide your family connections; it may even affect your job and your relationship with those who feel that it is wrong. Having said that, Benji, you can't allow the opinions of others to dictate your life choices. If you do, you will always find yourself pulled in two or more directions. I don't think that dating Heidi and maybe eventually marrying her is morally or ethically wrong. I don't believe that it is a violation of your Christian principles; however, mine is just one more opinion like everyone else's. Only God can direct you in the right way. You just have to seek His will in this matter. But I want you to know that I'll stand with you and support you in whatever He leads you to do."

"Dad, we've been praying about it but have not received His answer," Benji said. " What more can I do?"

Rusty reminded him that he still had school to complete and that both he and Heidi were extremely busy in their work and it wouldn't be fair to Heidi for them to marry under the present circumstances, but that when the time came, God would show him the way. "Thank you, Dad. You always help me to see things through but don't ever tell me what to do. You leave that to the Lord. Will you pray for us to know His will?"

"Certainly. You know, Benji," Rusty added, "your feelings for Heidi and hers for you are no secret; they show. All of us have seen it, but I really appreciate your restraint as you wait on God's answer. When He answers, you will know it."

Benji seldom saw Katherine anymore because they were so busy in their respective jobs, so when she called and asked for an appointment to see him, he made time on his calendar for her. Late in the afternoon she came in sporting her spiffy nurse's uniform and greeted him with a hug and took a seat in his office. She was as pretty as ever, except for the responsibility lines he could see forming on her face. "You look great," he said. "I'm so proud to have you as my sister." They talked about their work, and she told him about her plans to begin the senior day care center and some retirement cottages. He was impressed with her insight and long-range planning. And he was excited to tell her all that was going on in the student ministry.

When she got around to the purpose for her visit, she began, "Benji, I'm sure Heidi has told you that she and I have discussed the matter of your relationship with her, and that I was very adamant with my objections. I'm sorry I was so unyielding. After I've had time to look at it more objectively, now I think I was just jealous. I don't want to lose my brother to anyone, but I do want you to marry the girl God has for you. I know that I'm praying that someday I'll find someone like Dad that I can share life with and have a family together. As for the propriety of your relationship, who am I to say that it is right or wrong? I do not want to push you but neither should I try to restrain you. So what I'm trying to say is that only you can discern God's will for you. I know that you and Heidi are praying about this and will do the right thing. But I don't want either of you to base your decision upon what I think," Katherine said.

"Thank you, Katherine, for sharing that with me," Benji said. " Now I think you should go talk to Heidi about it. After all she is the one who received your advice and she will be relieved to hear what you've just told me."

CHAPTER 17

Heidi's requests had been accepted. The construction company had been formed and two fulltime carpenters and a helper had been hired. In fact, one of them, Bill, had been transferred from the cabinet shop to be a working manager. They had been assigned their first task – building a new office building that would display all three names: Clark's Woodworking; Jenson's Windows and Doors; and Master's Construction Company. Heidi had drawn a rough diagram of what she thought they needed and Rusty had approved it, so work began immediately.

Rusty wanted to expand the halfway house ministry. But since the population at both houses was at capacity that meant they would need to purchase another house. Rusty and Lauren discussed it and agreed to be looking for a building they could buy. A short time later they learned that an old plantation house with several acres of land south of town was for sale, so they drove out to see it and upon seeing it experienced the excitement of a child in a toy store. Rusty stood on the wrap-around porch and thought about all of the people who had crossed this threshold. The house was more than a hundred years old, so he could envision horses tied to the hitching posts that still stood on the front lawn. He imagined the first automobile to roll into the driveway. In his imagination the laughter of children came out on a breeze through open windows. Inside some old pieces of furniture remained, including a crude kitchen table around which a family might have sat and planned their day as they ate hot biscuits, smoked ham, and fresh eggs from their own chickens.

The history of this family might well have included unhappy events, Rusty thought, such as involuntary abortions, infant deaths, sickness and deaths in old age. But the house had, no doubt, seen many happy occasions too, such as marriages, parties, holiday festivities, and family activities. As they explored the house, on the first floor level, they found a large family room, no doubt called a parlor once upon a time, a spacious kitchen, a pantry as large as a typical bedroom, a formal dining room, a library which still had a few tattered books strewn around, an office, and a bathroom. Upstairs on the second level, they found four bedrooms with large walk-in closets, two bathrooms, and a sitting room. The curtains had rotted and hung in tatters exposing large windows through which one could look out over the flower garden and orchard and which, when opened, would allow a breeze in. Rusty and Lauren crept up the rickety stairs to the dusty attic which looked like the last of the Barrett family had left untouched when they vacated the house. Large trunks, discarded pieces of furniture, as well as some family heirlooms and pictures filled the space. The attic could easily be converted to two good-sized bedrooms, Rusty thought.

When they had finished exploring the house, Rusty's notes revealed that quite a bit of decay to the structure would have to be replaced; rooms would need to be divided or enlarged; central heat and air was needed; and the entire structure would have to be painted inside and out. The cost would be considerably more than the $100,000 they would have to pay for the house and acreage. In addition, a new administration was in office in the state which included a new person granting permits for halfway houses and overseeing their operation. Rusty had not met him, but he thought the permit would be as easy as it had been before, so he filed the necessary papers requesting the permit.

Weeks passed without a word from the capital. Rusty contacted his representative and state senator and was promised that they would look into it. Finally he went to the capitol city to see a Mr. Leblanc who, he had been told, was the new man in charge of the permits. It was almost noon before Leblanc's receptionist informed him that, "Mr. Leblanc will see you now, but he can allow you only fifteen minutes." When Rusty entered the office, Leblanc had his back to the door doing something at a credenza or pretending to. After a few minutes he turned and without introducing himself or offering his hand to shake said, "Hello, how may I help you?" Rusty explained his business, after which the official called his secretary and asked to see the Jenson file. While he perused it briefly,

Rusty got the impression that he knew all about it already and that he had already made his decision.

"Frankly Mr. Jenson, I don't believe we will be able to grant you another permit. You already operate two halfway houses and there are others in your area, so we don't need another one."

"Then why are we having to turn away people who are trying to get into ours?" Rusty asked.

"I don't know the answer to that, Sir."

Rusty felt sure there was more to the denial, so he said, "Mr. Leblanc, I like to be honest and straight forward, and I like for others to show me the same consideration. Tell me the real reason why we are being denied a permit."

"Well, off the record, the reports show that you are using the homes to promote your religion and push your beliefs on the residents; therefore, I am not going to issue you an additional permit," Leblanc admitted.

"What about our success? Most of our residents leave us to go on and become productive citizens." Rusty argued.

"Your request has been denied, Mr. Jenson. Now if you will excuse me your time has expired." Rusty was angry enough that he could have beaten Leblanc to a pulp, but he kept his anger under control and walked out without another word. However, while in the capital, he inquired at the governor's office and was told confidentially that Leblanc had the sole authority in the matter. Disappointed, he and Lauren drove home feeling that without an expensive lawsuit, they were defeated. Back in Winslow he sought the advice of his friend and attorney, who said, "Rusty, the state has its own attorneys and they don't mind spending lots of our tax money. They can draw litigation out so long that it would cost you a lot of money. I advise you to hold off on this. I know you are committed to doing God's will, but are you sure that this is His will or just your desire?" As Rusty hesitated to answer, he realized that he wasn't sure, so it would be wise to wait until he was certain.

"Thanks Mr. Albertson, you've been a great help," Rusty said, as he turned to leave.

That evening Lauren told Rusty that they simply could not allow that place to slip through their hands. If they couldn't get it for a halfway house then maybe they could buy it and restore it for themselves, she thought silently. She didn't voice her desire to Rusty, but she knew they could remodel it with much less renovation than would be required for a halfway house.

When Rusty, Lauren, and Marie had finished their dinner, read the Bible, and prayed, Lauren asked, "Rusty do you think we could buy that plantation house for ourselves and begin renovating it? When the construction crew has some idle time, they can work on it, and in a year or two we will be able to move into it." Rusty was surprised for he had no idea that Lauren would ever want to move from the house they had spent all of their married life in, where their children had grown up, and so many memories had been made.

"What are you two talking about?" Marie asked. They described the house to her and explained their failure to get a permit to open a new halfway house there. "Oh, that sounds interesting," she said. "My grandparents lived in a house like that, and I used to go there as a little girl and have such fun. I want to go see it tomorrow." Marie was as excited about the house as Rusty and Lauren were. She too had a dream; "It's too large for just the three of us, so maybe we could open one of those Bed and Breakfast homes. I would love to run it."

"Now hold on," Rusty said. "We may be getting the cart ahead of the horse. Let's take one step at a time." But the next day he contacted the owner of the house and inquired about buying it and learned there was another prospective buyer who was trying to raise the funds to buy it. When he told the ladies, they were so disappointed, but they agreed that if it was God's will they would get it, and they prayed to that end.

Two weeks later the owner called to say that the other buyer had backed out and that if they were still interested the house was available. They were, so Rusty went immediately to close the deal. That evening they drove to the house to look around and dream of what they could do to it. An old swing hung on the porch and the ladies eased down in it testing its strength and swung while Rusty sat on the top step. "Girls," he said, "let's agree now that if we get this place that we will dedicate it to God, and if we do open a B&B we will make it a ministry, and not let a visitor leave here without hearing a Christian witness."

Meanwhile, the construction crew had already completed the office building and begun on a building for the senior day care, which Katherine had named Happy Hours. It would house as many as twelve guests with ample room for them to have activities and recline for an afternoon nap. And Katherine was already pressing them to get it finished so they could begin on the retirement cottages which were to be built on land that had been purchased a short distance away. Initially only two were to be constructed to test the market; if the project succeeded, more would be added. Each one would have a carport, a covered patio and enough land for a small garden. That left Rusty and Lauren with plenty of time to plan what they would like do to the plantation house.

CHAPTER 18

With three different units in different locations, Katherine began to work out the logistics of sharing the responsibilities of workers. The same employee and equipment could be used to maintain the grounds. The janitorial staff at TLC could also clean the day care building and if needed the cottages. Meals prepared at the nursing home would be served at the day care center as well. Residents at the cottages could have a meal plan and receive the same meals if they desired. Administration for all three would be performed at the nursing home. Katherine was proving to be very efficient both as an administrator and at directing the nursing staff, so Lauren's presence was required less and less.

The senior day care center, Happy Hours, opened with lots of publicity. It was the first facility of its kind for miles around and the only one in a town the size of Winslow. An overflow crowd came for the open house and enjoyed the tour and refreshments. Six residents were signed up to use the service, just enough to test the planned program. So, with a competent staff in place, it opened for business the following week, and as the word spread, more people expressed an interest in this "ministry" to senior adults. Katherine could already envision the day when the building would have to be enlarged to accommodate more.

Rusty, Lauren, and Marie got busy planning the renovation of the plantation house. The idea of a B&B was growing on them, so they had investigated the requirements for permits, etc. and completed the necessary paper work. With the plans complete, they waited for the construction crew to get to them. However, they undertook some of the tasks themselves and enjoyed working together and seeing the changes completed. Rusty and Lauren decided to convert the library into the master bedroom for themselves and to provide bookcases in the family room for reading materials. Marie loved the view from the attic and requested it for herself. The exercise climbing the stairs would be good for her, she thought. That left the entire second floor for four guest rooms.

They learned that the house might qualify to be listed on the national registry of historic buildings, so they worked to verify the requirements for it. The primary things were the age of the building, its prominence, condition, and historical significance. Since one of the state's governors had been born there a hundred years earlier that was one positive qualification.

When President Franklin Delano Roosevelt established the Works Progress Administration (WPA) in 1935 to aid in the recovery from the Great Depression, more than three million participants would need to be housed in numerous facilities around the country as they built roads, bridges, public buildings, parks, and airport landing fields, so the owners of the planation graciously consented for one camp to be located on the plantation, and a tent city was there for its entire eight-year existence.

Then during World War II one of the seven hundred German Prisoner of War camps, housing a total of 425,000 prisoners was located on the outer edge of the property. Those factors plus the Jensons' plans to make few structural changes helped to qualify the home for the national registry. The process would take months and months before approval, but they knew they could wait.

Three months passed before the carpenters came to begin the lengthy task. As the work progressed, a retired plumber and his helper made repairs and upgraded the bathrooms and installed a treatment plant. They discovered that there was a deep well which, with a new pump and piping could provide water for the house as well as the lawn and garden. A retired electrician worked almost full time re-wiring the house, adding receptacles and fixtures. Lauren had found a lovely old chandelier to hang in the family room, and antique lamps for every room. Modern, yet old-fashioned looking equipment was installed in the kitchen.

It took a year to complete the renovation and get the designation as a national treasure. Then the townspeople were invited to an open house. They were greeted by a vintage sign on the front lawn introducing Hope Cottage B&B. Lauren and Marie greeted the guests wearing antebellum

...d them throughout the building. Rusty wore a butler's ...elcomed people to the house.

...his commitment to have a Christian witness, Rusty placed a ... with gospel tracts on it near the entrance. Then when everyone ...ied in the family room he spoke to the group thanking them for ...ing and sharing a little bit about their dream for the place. "The ...estoration of this old house will preserve important history. We've done as much as we could to retain its antebellum status, even to hanging pictures we found in the attic that are reminders of those who once lived here or their older family members. It will also allow guests to step back in time to a gentler period, less hectic than today. We've made a commitment that we would not allow anyone to leave here without hearing a Christian witness. Many of you knew me when I was a wild young man, but I'm not the same man I was, and I want you to know that it's because of Jesus Christ in my life. He has forgiven my sins, given me new life, and blessed me with a fine family and more blessings every day than I ever dreamed of. He loved me to Him, and He loves you too, and He wants to bless you with eternal life. If you haven't trusted Him, I urge you to call on Him and be saved. And if any of you are interested, I'll be happy to talk with you about it privately."

With the help of a computer-savvy person, they created a web page for the B&B and published it on the internet, and also ran advertisements in travel magazines, and area newspapers. The local tourist information center included them in their promotion of the area.

Gradually they were putting together a video that showed some of the history of the plantation that had once boasted a thousand acres of farmland and pasture. Soon they were enjoying guests regularly; some weekends all four bedrooms were occupied, and Marie provided the guests with delicious breakfasts before sending them on their way.

Their exuberance was soon chilled, however, when Mr. and Mrs. Adams, a lovely couple in their thirties, along with their ten-year-old son, Joel, came for a weekend. As soon as they had brought their luggage in and placed it in their room, Joel wanted to go outside and explore. His parents cautioned him to be careful and he promised to. But when he had not returned an hour later, they became concerned and all of them went searching for him. They called and looked over the whole place without finding him. Then Rusty spotted some disturbed weeds and went to investigate. What he discovered almost put him in shock; some rotted boards had broken through into an old abandoned well which he never knew was there. He feared the worst and called for the others. When they peered into the well it was as dark as night, so Rusty ran to get a powerful flashlight to shine into the depths of it. All they could see at the bottom was a tiny bit of red, and they knew that Joel had been wearing a red shirt. Their shouts into the well drew no response.

"Call 911 Rusty shouted and Lauren used her cell phone to report the crisis and to direct the emergency vehicles to their location. When they arrived and searched the depths of the well, they knew that someone had to go down into it. They called for the department's ladder truck and tied a strong rope to it and planned to use it to lower a man in and lift him out again. When they asked who would go down, before a fireman could volunteer Rusty spoke up, "Let me go." They put him in a harness and lowered him with a light. It took all of the rope to reach the muddy bottom, but when he saw Joel he feared the worst. Checking for a pulse, he found no trace of one. Joel had landed head first and was half buried in the mud. Rusty struggled to free him from the mud, then took him in his arms and called for them to pull him up. On the way up he prayed for the parents for he knew that it would be the worst tragedy of their young lives.

Mrs. Adams screamed when she saw her son and then fainted. Lauren rushed to her side to render aid, while Mr. Adams had to be restrained by the firemen.

When Mrs. Adams revived, she screamed at the Jensons, "You have killed my baby!" And the father began immediately to threaten the Jensons with a lawsuit. "You should have known that danger was there and done something about it" When the ambulance took the boy away, they quickly followed in their car. But the doctor could do no more than pronounce him dead. The hospital staff helped them to contact the funeral home in their home town, and even after they left Rusty did everything in his power to assist them: he prayed for them; he called but they refused to talk to him; and he contacted his insurance carrier and insisted that they be compensated to the limits of his liability coverage. Rusty, Lauren, and Marie drove more than a hundred miles to attend the funeral services and to visit with the distraught parents and return the luggage they had left behind. Mrs. Adams remained furious with them, but her husband told them before they left for home that he didn't blame them but that they were hurt so deeply that it would take time to heal. The mother told them that she didn't think she could ever forgive them. The Jenson family blamed themselves and as a result closed the doors to the B&B until further notice.

The well was filled that week, and three months later a memorial was erected to the memory of the deceased boy. The Jensons contacted Mr. and Mrs. Adams to inform them that a dedication of the memorial to Joel would be held at the unveiling of the memorial and invited them to come. The couple discussed it and decided that it might help them to heal if they attended and stayed at Hope Cottage again, so the Jensons opened the home to them as honored guests. They stood before the memorial located on the site of the abandoned well to say goodbye to their son. "If he had not been so adventurous this would never have happened," the father admitted. "Rusty and Lauren, we cannot blame you anymore," the mother offered. "You have been very kind and helpful to us, and we shall always count you among our friends. We hope you will open the Hope Cottage again so others can be blessed by coming here." With that the pall was lifted and they opened for business again after making sure there were no other hidden dangers on the place.

CHAPTER 19

Summer came and Benji went away to school again still uncertain about his relationship with Heidi. He didn't see her often and almost never alone. They didn't bring up the subject of their love for each other, but it was obvious to everyone who saw them together. Both of them made it a matter of prayer every day, and still they felt that God hadn't given them a definite answer. Benji had determined that he would complete his seminary training before taking any action and Heidi accepted that while refusing to allow any interest in another man. When he left Winslow, however, they agreed to write each other and talk by telephone every Friday night at 9:00. Sometimes those calls didn't end until after midnight.

When the summer session was over, Benji came home to Winslow to begin another hectic schedule at the university. He had made a decision to talk with his mother about Heidi, so he invited her to lunch and laid out the problem to her. "Benji, you are not telling me anything I haven't seen for months now. It's so obvious that you two are deeply in love. I'm sure that others may not see this as I do, but I don't see anything wrong with it. God gave us the ability to love everybody, but one person in a special way. He also directs us to that special person who is to be our mate, and he doesn't ask for the opinion of others. He knows what's best and He directs us to it. If you and Heidi do marry, God will give you the grace to deal with any repercussions that may come. I won't tell you what to do, but I will tell you to seek God's will only and whatever He leads you to do I will support. Heidi is such a lovely girl. What you need to do is try to see her without seeing your adopted sister and forget their connection. What would you do if she were not Katherine's sister?" Lauren probed wisely.

Benji knew what he had to do, what he couldn't keep from doing, but he still stuck to his plan to wait until he was finished with school. That evening he met Heidi after work for dinner to talk with her. "Heidi, it has been more than two years now since I asked you to date other guys. Have you found Mr. Right yet?"

"Yes, I have," she answered.

"What? I had no idea!" he exclaimed.

"He is sitting across the table from me right now. I'll never settle for anyone else, Benji, even if I have to remain an old maid for life. You're not going to get rid of me." Hearing her answer, Benji shared with her what his decision was and that it would be nine more months before they could move forward with their relationship.

"Oh, Benji," she cried. "Is it settled then? No more hoping; no more seeking God's will in the matter? In nine months we will be dating and planning a wedding."

"That's right."

"How have you reached this decision?" she asked.

"Well," Benji explained, "I've become convinced that God wouldn't have allowed us to love each other so if He couldn't allow us to become husband and wife. As hard as it would have been, I think I would not have done this if He had shone me that it was wrong."

"Benji, when we get to the car, will you kiss me to seal this decision?" Heidi asked.

"I can't wait to kiss you for the first time, the first of many, I might add."

Benji buried himself in his work at the student center and his studies, determined to complete the degree by the next May. And Heidi was overwhelmed with responsibility as she managed Clark's Woodworking and the other businesses. With little opportunity to be together, it seemed to both of them that the months dragged by, but the spring graduation finally arrived and Benji was awarded his degree in student ministry. And as soon as he was back home he called Heidi for a formal date and picked her up after work and they drove to the fanciest restaurant in town. Before dessert, he pulled a little square box from his pocket and knelt on one knee and asked Heidi to be his wife. She broke into tears, so she could only nod her acceptance. That very night they began planning for a wedding at the first of August which would hardly give them time to complete all the preparation.

Benji and Heidi had never had a disagreement or any kind of problems, but their love was about to be challenged. Jane, Benji's girl friend from years before, called and asked to see Benji, so he invited her to the ministry office for a 10:00 appointment. She arrived with a seven-year-old boy in tow. They greeted each other cordially. Benji had not seen her in more than seven years, but she looked like she had aged twenty. Drug abuse had taken its toll. "Who's this?" he asked, pointing to the child.

"Meet your son, Ken," she responded.

For a few moments, Benji was tongue-tied. "What are you talking about?" he demanded. "This can't be! Why haven't you told me before now?"

"I really wasn't sure who the father was, but if you will count up the time, you will see that it can be and is yours; besides, if you will look closely at Ken, you will see yourself," Jane explained.

"I'm sure there were other men. Before I accept responsibility we will have to do a paternity test," Benji insisted.

"Okay, but it has to be done soon."

"You've waited seven years; what's the rush now?" Benji inquired.

"I'm an addict," Jane confessed, "and in order to support my habit, I had to begin dealing and was finally caught and arrested. I'm out on bail now, but my trial is coming up in two weeks, and my lawyer has told me to expect to be sentenced to at least ten years in prison. I have no choice but to place Ken with someone else, so who better than his father? I'm willing to give up all claims to him because he needs a good father to raise him during these next ten or more years. Then when I'm released you will still have full custody."

"You've thought this through, haven't you? I have to tell you that it creates a real crisis for me; I'm the director of this student ministry, and I've just got engaged. To become an instant father may destroy it all," Benji worried aloud.

"I'm sorry, but in two weeks, Ken will be left on your doorstep. Can you reject your own flesh and blood? In the meantime we can get blood tests if you need the proof."

"I don't want to question you, Jane, but I have to be sure, so let's go for testing tomorrow," Benji suggested.

"Okay, but you will have to pick us up; I don't have transportation. Call and make the appointment and let me know when you will be there. We'll be ready," she promised.

With that, Jane got up, took Ken by the hand, and said, "We will see you tomorrow."

When Jane had gone, Benji called his doctor and asked for the blood tests the next morning and informed his student assistant that he was leaving for the day and that he might be late coming in the next day. Then he went home to wrestle with the problem. He knew that he would have to tell Heidi soon, but he would wait until he was sure before telling anyone. The state director and the local board of directors would have to know soon, too.

Benji went home remembering the scripture that states, "Be sure your sins will find you out." He thought all of that was behind him and that he had been fully forgiven, but the effects of his waywardness lingered to plague him. The next morning he drove to the address Jane had given him; it was one of those run-down, low-rent apartments. As promised, she and Ken were ready and he drove them to the doctor's office where in a few minutes the blood was drawn. "When will we know the results?" Benji asked.

"Tomorrow morning we'll have the type, but the DNA will take longer," the doctor explained.

Benji ached to talk to someone - Heidi, Rusty, Lauren, or Katherine – but he would wait through another restless night. Suddenly he realized that all he was thinking about was his own problems and what others would think, but what about the little boy? Whether he was the father and accepted his responsibility or not, there was a seven-year-old boy who would need a home in two weeks. Could he just accept a homeless boy and not tell anyone that this was his son? No, that would not be honest, he thought. "I'll just have to tell the truth and face the consequences," he muttered.

After a sleepless night, he called the doctor's office when it opened the next morning, but they were still waiting for the report to arrive from the lab, and promised to call him as soon as they had the results. An hour later the doctor called to say that there was a match of the blood type. "How reliable is that, doctor?" Benji asked.

"It's positive proof that there could be kinship. It won't prove you are the father conclusively, but it's certain enough that I can say he is your child. The only thing more accurate is DNA testing which we'll have in a few weeks."

Benji drove to Jane's apartment and woke her out of a drug-induced sleep to tell her what she already knew, and when he looked at Ken he could hardly deny it any longer.

"Okay," he said, "I accept responsibility and will take the boy and raise him as mine. Let me talk with an attorney and find out what legal steps we need to take, but what if you do not get the sentence you expect?"

"I want you to have him anyway. As much as I love him, I'm not a fit mother for him. Can you come get him the day before I go to trial?" Jane begged.

"Yes, I'll be here."

CHAPTER 20

Benji was in a daze; he couldn't believe what was happening. He just knew that he had to see Heidi, so without even calling he drove to her office. "Hello, handsome," she greeted him cheerfully.

"Hi" was all he could say.

"What's wrong," Heidi inquired. "You look like you haven't slept in days. Are you sick?"

"I'm sick, but not in the way you mean. I'm sorry, but I have to call off the wedding," he blurted out.

"What are you talking about? We've just started planning it. What do you mean we have to cancel it? Why?"

"It's a long story, Heidi, and I'd rather not tell you," Benji admitted.

"Oh, but you are not going to get off that easy," Heidi insisted. " Look, you've dropped this bombshell, and you are going to tell me why." Benji broke down crying and when Heidi saw the tears she knew that it was a difficult choice for Benji. She ran to him and took him into her arms to comfort him. After she released him, he was calmer, but she probed to get the answers she sought.

Benji confessed, "I have a seven-year-old son."

"No, it can't be true. You've never told me." Then Benji quietly told her the unbelievable story.

"Jane will be going to jail in two weeks and, as his father, I have to provide a home for Ken. I can't ask you to marry me under these conditions. I don't know how difficult this will be; I don't even know whether I'll have a job when this gets out. I can't ask you to become an instant mother," Benji said apologetically.

"I admit that this is quite a blow and I'm going to need some time," Heidi said. "I love you, Benji, but I don't know if I can accept this. Things just won't be the same now. I agree with you that it is best for us to at least postpone the wedding."

"I guess I'd better go," Benji said. But before he made it to the door, Heidi caught up with him and hugged him sympathetically. "I'll keep you posted," he said as he closed the door behind him.

Benji knew that he had to tell his family next. So he dragged himself into their house just as they sat down to dinner. They insisted that he join them, so he seated himself at the table and toyed with the food. "What's wrong, Benji?" Lauren asked.

"I'd rather not tell you, but I guess I have to. Jane came to see me a couple of days ago and brought our son." They sat quietly while he shared the whole story from the drug parties to the blood tests and Jane's upcoming trial. "I don't know what I'm going to do," he confessed. "But I have to accept him as my son and provide a home for him. He needs someone and it's my responsibility, so whatever the consequences I can't undo the past."

Rusty spoke first and offered to share Benji's burden and promised that whatever happened they would support him and stand by him in every way. Lauren rose and came around the table to hug him and express her love. Marie assured him that if he needed her to help with the child she was available.

"Son, you don't need to be alone tonight," Rusty said, "so you stay here with us tonight and we can talk this out and pray about it."

"I have to call Waylon Kennedy, the state director of student ministries and go talk with him tomorrow," Benji said.

"Call him tonight and see if you can make an appointment for tomorrow, and I'll go with you. You don't look like you need to be driving," Rusty offered.

When they arrived for the 11:00 appointment the director was jovial and happy to see Benji and Rusty. "I'm so glad to see you, but you said that this is urgent, so tell me what it is about, Benji." Benji told him the whole story and acknowledged that he was ready to accept the consequences.

"This could be a big problem for you, Benji, and we will need to get right on it. I think that it will be best if you take a leave of absence until this is resolved. I'll contact your local board and plan a meeting with them as soon as possible. I'll plan to meet with them first, but they may want to meet with you also. Do you agree, Benji?" he asked.

"Or course. Whatever we need to do, I'm ready," Benji assured him.

Waylon invited them to go to lunch and they went to a nearby cafeteria and sat through a solemn visit together. Benji shared that his plans to marry had been put on hold for the time being. Before parting they prayed for solutions to the problems this would create, and for Benji.

Having talked with everyone he needed to see immediately, Benji was more relaxed and he dropped off to a much-needed sleep as Rusty drove them home. The next morning Benji called Jane and woke her again to suggest that he needed to see Ken now to begin getting acquainted and bonding. She agreed and suggested that Benji bring food for a picnic and meet them in the park at noon. Ken was a personable little fellow and fully aware of what was happening. "Do you understand that I'm your father, and that you are going to be living with me soon?" Benji quizzed him.

"Yes, because my mom has to go away to jail for a long time. She says that I will live with you all the time now. I don't want her to go away, but she says she has to," Ken explained. Despite her personal problems and neglect of her own health, it appeared that she had provided very well for her son. They planned for Benji to pick up Ken the next morning and spend the day with him, so when Benji arrived at 9:00 Ken was ready to go. They went first to Benji's apartment for Ken to see where they would be living. After getting better acquainted, they went out to a fast food restaurant for hamburgers and fries which Ken loved. Then they drove to Heidi's office and Benji took Ken in to meet Heidi and Rusty, who happened to be in the office, and they both spent time getting to know the little boy.

Rusty told Benji about a new piece of equipment that had been added in the woodworking shop and asked him to go with him to see it. But thinking that the shop would not be a safe place for a seven-years-old, Benji asked Ken and Heidi if he could wait in her office and they both were pleased. As they walked toward the shop Rusty said, "Benji, you can't deny that boy. He looks too much like you at that age."

In the office Heidi engaged Ken in an enlightening conversation. She didn't want to pry, but she did want to know as much about this little fellow as possible. "Are you enjoying your day with Benji, Ken?" she asked.

"Do you mean my daddy?" he responded. It shocked Heidi to hear the question until he added, "Yes, I am. I've never had a daddy before and I'm glad I do now. When my mom goes away I'm going to be living with him all the time. He doesn't have a wife to be my mom, so I'll really miss Mom." Heidi had to turn her back to Ken and pretend to be busy at something to hide the tears in her eyes.

Benji and Rusty returned to find Heidi and Ken getting along well. She had given him a candy bar from her stash in the desk. Benji had introduced Rusty as his father, so Ken looked at him and asked, "If Benji is my daddy, what will you be?"

"I'll be your grandfather," Rusty responded. "And you can call me 'Granddad' if you want to. Say, I have an idea, why don't you and your dad go out to our house and stay for dinner? I'll call Marie and ask her to cook enough for the whole family. Then I'll call Katherine and Cathy and see if they can all come. Then Ken will get to meet all of his new family."

"Okay, that sounds good to me. What do you think, Ken?" Benji asked.

"Oh boy. I want to. But we need to call my mom and let her know for she will be expecting me home before then." They called but got no answer. "She's probably gone with her friends," Ken said.

When Benji and Ken arrived at the huge house, Ken's eyes were big for he couldn't believe the size of the place. "Is this where you lived when you were little?" he asked Benji. The new dad explained about the B&B and started to take his son inside. "Can we stay out here and run around first?" Ken begged. So they walked the grounds, exploring every nook and cranny. "Boy, I sure wish I lived in a place like this," he said.

"Well, you will get to spend a lot of time here, I promise. Now, let go inside and meet some people." Lauren and Marie met them at the door and Benji introduced them and tried to explain their relationship, but the only thing that Ken seemed to grasp was that Lauren was his grandmother.

"What will I call you," he asked Lauren.

"Well, let's see. What about 'Grammy?' How does that sound? And you can call this lady who is cooking you a good supper 'Grandmom.'" The word spread through the whole family and everyone came, Cathy, husband Sean, and their three children, Katherine, and Heidi. When the meal was served they all sat at the big table and Rusty offered thanks. It was obvious that Ken was not accustomed to prayer and Bible reading, but when they were finished, he remarked, "My momma prays some time when she's feeling real bad."

Ken wanted to see all of the house, so since there were no B&B guests, Marie offered to give him the grand tour including her space in the attic, which she dubbed the "Eagle's Roost." The boy was fascinated with everything. "I've never lived in a big house. We have to live in an apartment because my mom doesn't always have a job." The family soon learned that they didn't have to ask questions, for Ken was more than willing to tell everything as he talked incessantly.

As dark approached, Benji told everybody that he had to return Ken to his mother and they headed for the apartment. However, when they arrived Jane was not at home. "I know where the key is," Ken volunteered, and Benji realized that this was not the first time Ken was left alone. He knew that he couldn't leave the child and thought he would stay until she returned. But inside the apartment there was a note saying that Jane was away for the night and a request that Benji take Ken home with him. She promised to call when she was home again. "Good," Ken shouted, "I can spend the night with you. I won't have to stay here all by myself tonight."

For the next few days, Benji spent a good part of every day with Ken. But when Jane's trial date arrived, Benji went to give her a ride to the courthouse and she told Ken goodbye for she didn't want him going to the courtroom or seeing her taken away in handcuffs. She had packed Ken's few things in a cardboard box and discarded everything else. Benji dropped her off at the courthouse and drove Ken to leave him with Marie for the day. Then he returned to observe the trial proceedings. As expected Jane was given a ten-year sentence without benefit of parole. Before she was led away, Benji had a chance to tell her that he would bring Ken to visit but she adamantly refused. "I do not want him to see me there. He's yours. Your raise him! I'm not fit," but she left with tears streaming down her cheeks. Benji could not help but feel sorry for her.

CHAPTER 21

Waylon Kennedy called to inform Benji that a meeting with the board of directors was scheduled for Monday morning. "Frankly, Benji, I have to tell you that they already know about this and more. Your pastor 'friend,' Dr. Higgins has been busy on the telephone. He has called all of the members campaigning for your dismissal. I'd like you to come as an observer but sit silently unless you are called on to explain something. Can you do that?" Benji would endure an anxious weekend, but he and Ken visited his family, fished in the plantation pond, and made arrangements for Marie to keep Ken Monday. Although they sat with the Jenson family at church on Sunday, Benji could hardly concentrate on the sermon for thinking and praying about his own situation, but by the end of the service he decided that all he could do was leave it in God's hands and accept what He brought about.

Benji slipped into the meeting room Monday morning after the meeting had begun, and Waylon was reviewing the facts calling for their decision. Early in the meeting Dr. Higgins demanded that he be allowed to speak and was granted permission. "I love Benji and appreciate all he has done at the student ministry, but I also love the large number of students who are being affected and influenced by him. The Lord has told me that this young man has to be dismissed as the ministry director. We cannot allow him to continue to teach and lead our young people because of two things. First, it has now come to light that he has fathered an illegitimate child with a known drug addict and drug pusher. He has now brought this child into his home and will be exposing this sorry mess to our precious young people. Second, he is engaged to and plans to marry his step sister. That's incest, brethren. Oh, I know that the wedding has been postponed but as soon as this other has quieted down they'll re-schedule it, no doubt. Gentlemen, you have to take a stand and expeditiously get rid of him." With that Higgins returned to his seat staring as Benji with hate in his eyes.

"Gentlemen, you've heard these charges. Now what do you have to say?" Kennedy asked.

Immediately one of them spoke up and said, "I think we need to hear from Benji and see what he has to say." A chorus of "Amens" rose from the group.

"Benji, would you like to speak to this matter?" Waylon asked.

"I will if that's what you want," he responded. First, Benji apologized that they were put in this precarious situation. He expressed his sincere regret for some things that had taken place in his life while he was in a backslidden condition seven years earlier. "I'm guilty of wrongdoing then, and I've taken the scriptural steps of repenting and asking God's forgiveness and the forgiveness of my church and others that I hurt. But I assure you that with God's help I've walked a straight and narrow path since." Benji then told them the entire story of his past and how he came to know about his son and why he would have Ken. "He is my son, and I will not shirk my responsibility to him."

Having explained about Ken, Benji tackled the second issue, explaining that Heidi was not in any way a blood relative of his. He went through the story of her past and told how his parents came to have Katherine and what prompted Heidi's move to Winslow. He also explained the long struggle he had gone through before accepting what he believed was God's will for him and Heidi and that the wedding had been postponed, if not cancelled.

Higgins interrupted Benji's explanation to say, "You're just trying to save your job, Benji. Why don't you just resign and settle this whole matter?"

Patiently, Benji replied, "I've prayerfully considered it, Sir, but the reason I haven't is because God has called me to this ministry at this university. To quit it would be to reject His will. As for the job, I would not be out of work; there are any number of opportunities for me to work either in one of my family's businesses or elsewhere, but this is what God's called me to do. Of course I'm concerned about my work, about my reputation, the effect of this on my family, but by far my greatest concern is for the students. I do not wish to do anything that would affect them negatively."

Just then the door opened and Pastor Williams, now Pastor Emeritus of First Church, rushed in and spoke: "Excuse me gentlemen for barging into your meeting, but I just heard about this gathering and I feel I have to speak to the issue. I've known the Jenson family and been their pastor since Benji's father came back here as a young man, and I can tell you that there is not a more committed Christian family in Winslow, including mine and Dr. Higgins' families, I might add. I know about Benji's backsliding and his restoration, and I am also very familiar with the ministry he has led so successfully here. I urge you to pray long and hard lest you make a rash decision that would be a mistake."

Chairman Mark Hendrix, who was moderating the meeting, asked if any of the board members had questions to ask Benji and none did. Then he surprised the guests by saying, " Bros. Higgins and Williams, thank you for coming to share your wisdom today, but you are excused now. And Benji we will excuse you also and allow the board the opportunity to discuss this in private. Higgins had nothing to say to Benji, but rushed to his car, but Dr. Williams came and put his arms around Benji and said, "Don't worry, Son. God's going to work this out. You are too good a man to be defeated by these things. Remember, I'm praying for you." With those encouraging words, he was gone.

Benji never knew what was said in the meeting. In fact, he didn't want to know. However, Mark called him later in the day and advised him that the board members wanted a week to pray and think about their decision. So it was agreed that they would meet at the First Church dining hall for breakfast the next Monday morning at 7:00. Benji agreed and promised himself that he would not spend the week in worry but leave the matter in God's hands and accept their decision. He planned to spend the week buying school clothes and supplies for Ken and enrolling him in the local school. Ken was excited about going to a new school away from the rowdy neighborhood he had lived in with his mother. He asked Benji if he could write to Jane, and even though Benji didn't have a mailing address, they decided they would send it in care of the prison where she was serving her time. Benji helped Ken to write the touching letter but allowed Ken to express his thoughts in his own words. He told Jane all he and his dad had done and about his new clothes and school. Last, he told her that he loved and missed her.

University classes were scheduled to begin in a week, so with Benji out of the office, Sam Cox, the former director, came back to try to fill in for him and get everything ready for the beginning of the semester. Monday morning Benji walked into the dining hall humbly, but with his head held high. Every board member came to greet him personally and wish him well. Obviously they had communicated during the week and made a decision. When the chairman rose to speak, he first thanked Benji for the excellent work he had done at the student ministry and assured him of their support for the future. "We've investigated the charges against you and admit that we wish you didn't have this skeleton in the past and hoped that marriage to Heidi, when understood by all involved, could be seen as right and ethical. Benji, our unanimous decision is to re-instate you as director of the student ministry beginning immediately. However, as you know there are questions being raised about you worthiness, so we are going to put you on a one-year probation and hope that in that time this storm will blow over. Will you agree to those terms, Benji?"

"Gladly," he responded. "And I thank you for the professional way that you have handled this sticky situation. You have been very supportive. Whatever your decision might have been, I would have been confident that you made it as mature, prayerful Christians, who, like me, want the very best for our students." After a warm round of applause and back-slapping, Benji announced that he would go and arrange for Ken's care and be in the office ready to work in an hour. He called Marie who was delighted to keep him for the day. But before Benji could get away from the church his cell phone was ringing constantly as family members and close friends called to find out the decision and to wish him well. Benji had left Ken in an empty classroom at the church with plenty to keep him busy and ordered him to stay there until he returned, so he retrieved him and delivered him to Hope Cottage.

When Benji arrived at the office there were several students who had come early for the semester and a number of faculty members present to welcome him back and assure him of their support. During his time off Benji had already outlined his plans for the semester, so he began the process of putting them into motion. He decided that he would not voluntarily share the turmoil he had been going through with the students.

After all, many of them were from out of town and would know nothing of what had taken place, and he felt they were better off not knowing.

When Heidi went to visit her mother the next time, Nancy asked if they could talk about something very serious. She told Heidi that she had heard about Benji's child and that the wedding was postponed. "You remember that when you asked me about your dating him, I spoke against it, but I have come to accept the fact that since you are in no way related that there is nothing wrong in your marrying. I also understand the circumstances under which Ken was born, and I admire Benji for taking responsibility for his child regardless of the repercussions. However, I don't agree with canceling the wedding. Benji is still the same man, the man you love, so what are you going to do about it?"

"Mom," Heidi responded, "I do love Benji, and I want to marry him as much as I ever did. But you know that it was he who postponed the wedding. I think it was because he was afraid that I might not want to marry him under the circumstances. However, I think it was a good idea. My feelings for him have not changed, but my image of him as 'Mr. Perfect' has been shattered, So I don't think we should enter into marriage as long as there is a shadow of doubt hanging over us. The problem is not with Benji but with me; I don't have him on the same pedestal as I did, and I'm afraid of what affect that might have."

"Heidi, you understand that you were unrealistic in what you thought of Benji," Nancy responded. "He isn't some god, nor is he perfect. I believe that he is as fine a young man as you will find, But, like all of us, he has a past that was not always so perfect; he is still human. Do you think any less of me now that you know about my past? Don't let this twist in your life rob you of happiness. Think about this objectively and pray about it and rebuild your relationship with Benji." As a result of Nancy's advice, Ken, Benji, and Heidi spent the next Saturday together at the restored plantation, where they romped, fished, and watched the sunset. Benji and Heidi said little about their relationship but both knew that while it was being repaired the future was in no way certain.

CHAPTER 22

As the fall semester began at the university, the student ministry got off to a flying start. Many students were returning, but a new crop came also. Benji had planned an assembly the first week for the students and staff to get acquainted or re-acquainted. He would outline their plans for the semester and visit with them over refreshments. When Benji finished his prepared talk, he asked if anyone had questions, and a scowling student stood and said, "I do. My pastor said that you have an illegitimate son and that you are planning to marry your stepsister and that you should be fired. What do you have to say to that?"

Benji calmly responded: "Yes, I know that Dr. Higgins is saying that and campaigning for my ouster." With that acknowledgement, Benji very candidly explained about a son who was a product of a time when he used drugs and alcohol seven years before and that Heidi was no relation to him except the twin sister of his adopted sister. The heckler kept trying to interrupt until his fellow students stopped him, saying, "We thought you said you want to hear what he has to say. Will you be quiet and listen or leave?" Benji explained the probationary conditions of his service and encouraged the students to keep an eye on his life and service for the next year as well and make up their minds about his worthiness to serve. "If at any time you feel that I am wrong in my life or teaching, please let me know."

"Can you bring your son and fiancé here to let us meet them?" a young lady asked.

"Yes, I want you to meet them, so I'll bring them next week." The next week the girls were smitten with Ken and showed him lots of attention. Some of the boys had him playing table tennis before the evening was over, and the guys especially were impressed by Heidi's beauty and personality. Before the evening was over, most of the students had expressed their approval of Benji as well as with Ken and Heidi. As Benji and Heidi talked later, he asked, "Heidi, now that the storm has subsided, can you and I begin to thinking about starting over?"

Heidi answered," Maybe; we'll see."

Ken adjusted well to his new home environment as well as his school, and he loved going to Hope Cottage when he had the opportunity. However, he missed his mother and cried himself to sleep every night. Benji never pumped him for information about his mother, but in time he shared more and more about what he had been exposed to with her. For example, he asked Benji if he ever had a woman to come spend the night with him, then told him that Jane often had male visitors overnight and how he would have to prepare his own breakfast and get himself ready for school while they were still asleep.

Benji came to understand some of the trauma that Ken had experienced and that he needed some professional help to overcome its effect. So he arranged for counseling sessions with Dr. Sarah Blankenship, a child psychologist. She encouraged Ken to open up and share his feelings about his mother and the changes in his life. However, after weeks of therapy, he still cried for his mother and experienced difficulty adjusting.

The student ministry was very successful that year, and Benji was well accepted. In fact, the pastors of the city signed a letter addressed to the board voicing their approval of him and pledging their support for him. And secretly the students circulated a petition before the summer break asking that he be given a permanent status as their director. So when the board met, despite Pastor Higgins' objections, Benji's probationary role was removed and he was commended for his lifestyle and work ethic.

Benji and Heidi had seen each other regularly during the nine months since their upheaval, but their future was still uncertain. Heidi knew that Ken was still clinging to his mother and worried that he could not accept her. Benji, however, felt that the problems could be worked out but he didn't want Heidi to proceed with their relationship until she was sure of her own feelings.

One Saturday the three of them had planned a day together. They would spend the day at Hope Cottage; then Benji and Heidi were going to dinner together. The day was filled with fun activities, and late in the afternoon Heidi and Ken sat alone on the pier at the pond fishing and talking. Suddenly Ken turned to her and asked, "Heidi, will you be my mom?" She could barely hold back the tears as she remembered the seven years he had lived without a good mother and that now he was completely separated from her. He needed Heidi.

"Yes," she answered, "I'll be glad to be your mom, if you'll give me a big hug."

Ken got up from his seat and rushed to her and fell into her arms and they hugged each other until the tears stopped. Then they picked up their fishing gear and walked hand-in-hand to the big house. Neither spoke of their experience on the pier, but Heidi rushed to get herself ready for her date with Benji.

Benji, dressed in tan slacks and a navy blazer, met Heidi wearing her best dress in the family room and, after saying goodbye to the family, drove to an Italian restaurant, where a violinist played romantic music on Saturday nights. After a delicious meal, Benji took Heidi's hand across the table and asked, "Heidi, will you have me for your husband?" Tears flooded her eyes and she nodded yes, and he took the same ring he had given her before from his pocket and slipped it on her finger.

"That's the second romantic proposal I've had today," Heidi said, "so how can I possibly refuse?"

EPILOGUE

The Jenson family will continue to grow both in number and maturity. Although their faith is strong, it will be challenged in ways they never expected. Ken will be both a blessing and a problem for the young couple who try to mold his young life in the right way. Jane will be released from prison early and wage a legal battle to regain custody of her son, and child support along with him. Benji will lose his life in a horrific accident, and Heidi will be obsessed with her search for the cause of it, and eventually be successful with her investigation. Lauren will always be the unwavering support others need. In the coming years, the offspring of Rusty and Lauren will demonstrate clearly that indeed the acorn doesn't fall far from the tree.

CPSIA information can be obtained
at www.ICGtesting.com
Printed in the USA
BVHW081923280623
666441BV00005B/1103